Cassie tried to dispel some of her nervousness, smothering the wave of awareness that was making every female nerve ending stand at attention.

Beau was just a man, for goodness' sake. She'd dealt with many men in her life. There was certainly no reason to get all flustered every time this one looked at her.

Still, there was something very different about Beau that made her very aware of her own feelings and emotions. It was just a tad unnerving, since she truly thought herself immune from *any* kind of man.

Her experience with Sofie's father had left a bitter taste in her mouth and scared her off all men. As far as she was concerned, she couldn't trust her own judgment when it came to men, so she simply kept her distance. Besides, she was far too busy trying to support herself and her daughter to worry about impressing some man or squeezing time out of her hectic life to accommodate him.

But now, with Beau
back on her usual ro
not, she *needed* his
So she was going to
Sofie's needs ahead
jeopardize anything
No matter how charming he was.

Dear Reader,

April is an exciting month for the romance industry because that is when our authors learn whether or not their titles have been nominated for the prestigious RITA® Award sponsored by the Romance Writers of America. As with the Oscars, our authors will find out whether they've actually won in a glamorous evening event that caps off the RWA national conference in July. Of course, all the Silhouette Romance titles this month are already winners to me!

Karen Rose Smith heads up this month's lineup with her tender romance *To Protect and Cherish* (#1810) in which a cowboy-at-heart bachelor becomes a father overnight. *Prince Incognito* (#1811) by Linda Goodnight features another equally unforgettable hero—this one a prince masquerading as an ordinary guy. Nearly everyone accepts his disguise except, of course, our perceptive heroine who is now torn between the dictates of her head…and her heart. Longtime Silhouette Romance author Sharon De Vita returns with *Doctor's Orders* (#1812), in which a single mother who has been badly burned by love discovers a handsome doctor just might have the perfect prescription for her health and longtime happiness. Finally, in Roxann Delaney's *His Queen of Hearts* (#1813), a runaway bride goes from the heat and into the fire when she finds herself holed up in a remote location with her handsome rescuer.

Happy reading!
Sincerely,

Ann Leslie Tuttle
Associate Senior Editor

Please address questions and book requests to:
Silhouette Reader Service
U.S.: 3010 Walden Ave., P.O. Box 1325, Buffalo, NY 14269
Canadian: P.O. Box 609, Fort Erie, Ont. L2A 5X3

DOCTOR'S ORDERS

SHARON De VITA

SILHOUETTE Romance ®

Published by Silhouette Books

America's Publisher of Contemporary Romance

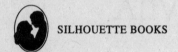

SILHOUETTE BOOKS

ISBN 0-373-19812-4

DOCTOR'S ORDERS

Copyright © 2006 by Sharon De Vita

Books by Sharon De Vita

Silhouette Romance

Heavenly Match #475
Lady and the Legend #498
Kane and Mabel #545
Baby Makes Three #573
Sherlock's Home #593
Italian Knights #610
Sweet Adeline #693
**On Baby Patrol* #1276
***Baby with a Badge* #1298
***Baby and the Officer* #1316
†*The Marriage Badge* #1443
††*Anything for Her Family* #1580
††*A Family To Be* #1586
My Fair Maggy #1735
Daddy in the Making #1743
Doctor's Orders #1812

Silhouette Special Edition

Child of Midnight #1013
**The Lone Ranger* #1078
**The Lady and the Sheriff* #1103
**All It Takes Is Family* #1126
†*The Marriage Basket* #1307
†*The Marriage Promise* #1313
††*With Family in Mind* #1450
††*A Family To Come
       Home To* #1468
Daddy Patrol #1584
Rightfully His #1656
About the Boy #1715

Silhouette Books

The Coltons
I Married a Sheik

**Lullabies and Love
†The Blackwell Brothers
††Saddle Falls
*Silver Creek County

SHARON DE VITA,

a former adjunct professor, is a *USA TODAY* bestselling, award-winning author of numerous works of fiction and nonfiction. Her first novel won a national writing competition for Best Unpublished Romance Novel of 1985. With almost three million copies of her novels in print, Sharon's professional credentials have earned her a place in *Who's Who in American Authors, Editors and Poets* as well as the *International Who's Who of Authors*. In 1987, Sharon was recipient of *Romantic Times BOOKclub*'s Lifetime Achievement Award for Excellence in Writing. Sharon and her husband, a retired military officer, currently make their home in the Southwest; they have four grown children and look forward—eagerly—to grandchildren. Sharon is hard at work on her next book.

To all who've been touched by Hurricane Katrina, good thoughts and prayers are with you, as well as with our heroic men and women in uniform who once again have stepped up to the plate and helped those who can't help themselves. I'm forever grateful to live in a country where help is always—always just a helping hand away.

Chapter One

S*omething was wrong.*

Cassie Miller's version of a mother's "early warning system" squealed in alarm as she glanced out the large plate glass window of her beauty salon, scanning Main Street and the crowd of kids for her six-year-old daughter, Sofie.

School had let out almost half an hour ago, and kids bundled in heavy winter clothes romped along the snow-packed street, dodging fresh snowflakes, ignoring the frigid cold, laughing and joking, grateful to be set free for another day.

But Sofie wasn't with them, Cassie realized nervously. The school was less than two blocks away, and her twelve-year-old nephew, Rusty, was supposed to walk Sofie from school to the shop every day after school.

But they were now almost half an hour late.

And it wasn't like Rusty or Sofie to just not show up or to not call if they were going to be late. Both were incredibly bright, responsible kids and knew the rules and how their mothers' worried about them.

Something was wrong.

Being a single parent, Cassie had worked hard to curb her instincts to overprotect her precious only child, but Sofie was a smart little girl who'd never given her a moment's worry.

Until now.

Cassie would have closed the shop and gone looking for Sofie herself, but she still had one more appointment this afternoon. She had just purchased the salon and was trying to garner all the business she could, and closing in the middle of the day without notice wasn't exactly a sound business practice.

Nervously gnawing on her lip, Cassie forced herself to take a deep breath. *Okay, Cass, get a grip here,* she scolded herself, closing her eyes for a moment to calm down. *Sofie's fine.*

She was worrying needlessly. After all, Cooper's Cove, Wisconsin, was the real-life version of Mayberry where everyone knew everyone else, and where she herself had grown up.

The move back home to Cooper's Cove a month ago hadn't been impulsive, Cassie reminded herself, and Sofie had been as excited about the move as she.

It was a new beginning for both of them, a chance to come home, to be near family, to set down roots, and for

Cassie to finally have a chance to realize her long-held dream of owning her own business.

It had been a well thought-out, intricately planned and perfectly executed move. She wasn't a woman who *ever* leapt before she looked, at least not anymore.

She'd leapt once, when she was young and naive and didn't know any better, and had nearly been done in by the pitfalls and perils of jumping so blindly. It wasn't likely she was ever going to do *that* again.

Feeling unbearably edgy when there was still no sign of Sofie after another few moments, Cassie rubbed her damp hands down her beige-and-brown uniform, then walked to the empty receptionist desk and picked up the phone.

She'd just started to dial the number for her cousin Katie, who was Rusty's mother and worked in the newspaper office several doors down, when she heard the roar of an engine out front.

Cassie glanced up in time to see a hot little red sports car zoom to the curb and come to an abrupt stop. She frowned. Expensive little red convertibles weren't exactly the norm in Cooper's Cove, and they certainly didn't roar down Main Street in the middle of the afternoon. Especially when there were tons of school kids out and about during near blizzard winter conditions.

Unless something was wrong.

Trying to curb her growing attack of nerves, Cassie's eyes widened when one of the winged doors glided open and Dr. Beau Bradford, the town pediatrician, emerged. Unconsciously, Cassie's lips thinned in displeasure.

Although she and the doctor had both grown up in Cooper's Cove, he had been several years ahead of her in school and they'd never met until last month, when she'd brought Sofie into his office for her school physical.

He'd also been at Aunt Louella's wedding to Mayor Hannity last month, Cassie remembered with a scowl, thinking of how charming and solicitous the good doctor had been. There was something about Dr. Bradford, something in those intense blue eyes and aristocratic dark good looks, that simply got on her nerves.

Dr. Beau, as everyone called him, wasn't just the town pediatrician, he was also the only heir to the Bradford plastics dynasty. He and his aging, eccentric uncle lived in a crumbling old fortress-like house on the edge of town.

Apparently the handsome young doctor also did some moonlighting as the town Romeo, Cassie remembered with another scowl. Tales of his romantic adventures had kept the gossips in Cooper's Cove busy for many a wash and set this past month, not to mention during the weekly bingo nights at the town hall.

The good doctor was rich, gorgeous and, according to Cooper's Cove lore, very experienced.

As far as Cassie was concerned, he was cut from the same soiled, spoiled cloth as Sofie's irresponsible father had been. And the last thing Cassie needed in her life was another rich, reckless man masquerading as an adult. The mere thought infuriated her.

So what on earth was he doing here, she wondered, her scowl deepening.

Cassie wasn't certain why, but she watched in fascination as he walked around to the other side of the car and opened the passenger door.

"Oh my word!" Cassie's panic went into overdrive when her six-year-old daughter stepped out of the car.

Bundled up for the winter weather, Sofie looked like a little woolen Weeble struggling to walk and keep her balance at the same time.

Cassie's heart did a quick stutter step. She slammed the telephone receiver down and skirted the receptionist desk to head for the front door, her heart now hammering in fear.

Without bothering to grab her coat, she yanked open the door, nearly recoiling from the arctic blast of cold air that hit her.

"Sofie!" Trying to contain her panic, Cassie rubbed her hands up and down her chilled arms as a myriad of horrible thoughts flashed through her mind. "What's wrong?" She reached for her daughter, all but dragging her through the doorway. "Are you hurt, honey? Sick?" Cassie demanded, alarm tingeing her words as she ran her hands up and down her daughter, checking for fever or injuries, wanting to assure herself Sofie was safe and sound and in one piece.

"No, Mama," Sofie said solemnly, glancing up at her from under the red woolen hat that drooped down her forehead and nearly covered her big brown eyes. "I'm not hurt," Sofie said, giving her cap a shove upward with a red mittened fist. "And I'm not sick, either."

"Then why did Dr. Bradford bring you home?" Cassie demanded. Confused, her gaze went from Sofie to Dr. Beau. She hadn't even noticed he'd followed them inside.

He was standing just inside the salon, tall and broad enough to almost fill the doorway, still wearing his cashmere overcoat and his expensive, designer wool scarf. Heavy leather gloves covered his large hands, and his inky black hair was windswept and dotted with fresh snowflakes that glistened as they melted.

Her gaze met his and she immediately felt as if she were

drowning in a calm, blue lagoon. There was something dangerous about his eyes…. If a woman wasn't careful, those blue eyes could just suck her in, making her blind and oblivious to reality.

She'd already had one life-altering turn with a slick, charming man, Cassie thought in annoyance, stiffening her resolve. She wasn't seventeen any longer, and she'd already learned her lesson…about men, life and just about every other pitfall in between.

"Will someone please tell me what the devil is going on?" Exasperated, her gaze went from Dr. Bradford back to her daughter. "Sofie, why are you so late? And why did Dr. Bradford bring you home if you're not hurt or sick? And where's Rusty? You know you're supposed to walk here with him every day after school, don't you?"

"Yes, Mama," Sofie all but whispered, staring down at the toes of her bright yellow Big Bird boots.

"And you know better than to get into a car with someone without my permission, don't you?" Cassie's gaze searched her daughter's face, but Sofie's chin merely drooped and she avoided her mother's eyes.

"Sofie." Gently, Cassie lifted her daughter's chin. "Sweetheart, when you didn't come home from school on time, Mommy got very, very worried. I was afraid something terrible had happened to you."

"Something…terrible…did happen, Mama," Sofie mumbled softly, glancing up at her mother through dark lashes glistening with tears. "At school."

Cassie's heart did another stutter step. "What happened, sweetheart?" she asked quietly, stunned by the stark sadness on her daughter's face.

Sofie sniffled, again staring down at the toes of her

bright yellow boots. "The kids at school…they laughed at me when I told them I'd seen red rain and that I was gonna do something real good for the science fair." Sofie lifted stricken, tear-filled eyes. "They called me a liar and then they laughed at me."

"They called you a liar and laughed at you?" Cassie repeated, stunned. Sofie had been bubbling over with excitement all week about the upcoming science fair. Science was her passion and had been ever since a former neighbor, a retired professor, had sparked her interest in the solar system.

For Cassie, a woman who had dropped out of school in her senior year to give birth, then had gone back to school at night just to get her G.E.D., the mere *concept* of scientific theories was a bit terrifying. But not for her brave, fearless, *brilliant* little girl.

"I'm so sorry, sweetheart." Gathering her daughter close, Cassie went down on one knee so she was eye level with Sofie. She swallowed the lump in her throat, and lifted Sofie's drooping chin. "It's not fun to be laughed at, honey. Or to be called names. Especially by your friends." Cassie pushed down Sofie's muffler so she could talk. "Now, tell me, sweetheart, why did the kids laugh at you?" Cassie smoothed away the stray strands of black hair that were clinging to her daughter's rosy, wind-whipped cheeks and smiled her encouragement.

Sofie swallowed, then swiped her nose with her fuzzy red mittens before answering. "Because…because…they say I'm…a brainiac, Mama," Sofie said, as tears flooded her eyes again.

"A *brainiac?*" Cassie repeated, and Sofie's little head bobbed up and down.

"The kids tease me 'cuz they say I'm too smart." Sofie rubbed her fuzzy red fists against her teary eyes. "They don't like me, Mama," Sofie wailed, sobs shaking her slender shoulders as she threw herself against her mother, hanging on for dear life. "They don't like me so that's why I was running away."

Her daughter's words had fear siphoning the blood from Cassie's head, nearly making her dizzy. "You were…running *away?*" Cassie repeated, trying to keep the shock out of her voice so she wouldn't upset Sofie further. But her knees were knocking now, nearly as hard and fast as her heart.

"Yes, Mama, but Dr. Beau found me." Sofie swiped her nose again, then peeked at her mother from under her drooping red cap. "And he told me about the first-grade rule."

Cassie merely blinked at her daughter. "The first-grade rule?" she repeated dully, glancing up at the doctor in confusion.

"Yes, Cassie," Dr. Beau confirmed with an encouraging wink and a smile. "The Cooper's Cove first-grade rule. I'm sure you were told about it when you registered Sofie for school?" he prompted, one brow lifting in expectation as his blue eyes twinkled at her.

"Uhm…yes, I'm sure I was," Cassie said with a slow nod, not sure of any such thing, but playing along anyway. "But I'm afraid I've…uh…forgotten it," she admitted, glancing up at him with a wan smile.

"That's perfectly understandable," he said, taking several steps deeper into the salon. As he pulled off his heavy leather gloves and shoved them in his pocket, he flashed Cassie and Sofie a dazzling smile. "The Cooper's Cove first-grade rule says all first graders have to tell their parents *before* they run away. It's a school rule, right, Sofie?"

"Yeah, it's a rule," Sofie admitted with a heavy sigh and Cassie nearly smiled in relief. Her gaze met Beau's and in it she saw humor, kindness and understanding, three things that surprised her coming from him.

"We didn't want to break any rules, now did we, Sofie?" he continued, and Sofie shook her head firmly.

"Uh-uh, Dr. Beau," Sofie said, scrabbling at a wad of long tangled black hair sticking to her face.

"I phoned Katie at the newspaper and told her I was driving Sofie here so neither she nor Rusty would worry."

"Thank you," Cassie muttered with a nod, still a bit shell-shocked.

Almost everyone in town knew everyone else's familial relationships. It was just part of small town life. Her mother, Gracie, and her Aunt Louella were sisters and partners in the Astrology Parlor a few doors down on Main Street. Katie was Aunt Louella's daughter, and Rusty was Katie's twelve-year-old son.

"Mama?" Sofie tugged on her mother's hand, then yanked off her cap, shoving her flyaway hair from her face with a fist. "Dr. Beau drove me here so I could tell you I was gonna run away." Sofie scowled suddenly. "But I think I gotta go to the bathroom first." Sofie shoved her hat at her mother, then crossed her legs and began bouncing up and down. "I gotta go *now,* Mama."

"Go, honey, go," Cassie urged, hurriedly helping to unwrap her daughter from her mound of winter clothing. "I'll be right here when you come out."

The moment Sofie was out of earshot, heading toward the back room where the restroom and the small lunch room were located, Cassie turned to Beau.

"I don't know what to say," she admitted honestly as she

set Sofie's winter coat down on one of the empty salon chairs. "Except…thank you." She hesitated, a chill skating over her skin. "If you hadn't found her, I don't know what would have happened."

Sofie had been running away.

Pure, unadulterated fear settled into an icy pit in Cassie's stomach. She simply couldn't bear to think about what might have happened if Beau hadn't found Sofie.

"You're welcome," Beau said with a smile. "I close the office early on Wednesday," he explained, "and I just happened to be driving down Main Street when I saw Sofie trudging along all by herself." He loosened his cashmere overcoat and stepped closer. "I knew something was wrong because I didn't figure you were the type to let your six-year-old go wandering around town by herself."

"No, of course not," Cassie said, fighting the instinct to step back away from him. It was foolish, she knew, especially considering how kind he'd been, but she couldn't help it. The man made her incredibly twitchy and nervous. He was just too charming, good-looking, and a tad too slick and smooth for her comfort. Everything about him was a painful reminder of Sofie's father, right down to his fancy, expensive sports car. The painful similarities simply irritated her and reminded her of her youthful inexperience and naivete.

"Pretty fast work about the first-grade rule," Cassie admitted, forcing herself to meet his gaze and be polite.

Beau shrugged away the compliment. "Dealing with kids every day, you have to learn to be quick and to think on your feet," he said, watching her carefully.

He'd been right about her the first time he'd met her, he mused, letting his gaze slide over her in pure masculine appreciation. She didn't like or trust him. She'd made that very clear. It wasn't the usual response he got from women and although he hadn't a clue why she felt that way it amused him to no end.

What he didn't know was if it was just *him,* or men in general, that Cassie Miller had a problem with. If his uncle had his way, all the single women in Cooper's Cove would be lining up outside Beau's office door, taking numbers for a chance to become the next heir-bearer for the future generation of Bradfords. Compared to that, Cassie Miller's apparent prickliness and standoffishness were more than just a bit…intriguing.

And that was saying nothing about how attractive she was with glossy black hair that fell like a dark halo to her shoulders, and gorgeous creamy skin that begged to be stroked. But then again, he'd always had a weakness for petite, slender women who looked fragile and frail, but were really built and backed with steel.

When she'd brought Sofie in for her physical, his attempts to be friendly had fallen on tin ears. And not just that day in his office, he remembered, but later, at her aunt Louella's wedding as well. He'd tried to make pleasant, polite conversation while Cassie had merely stared at him coolly, making it clear she didn't think he was either pleasant or polite…and that she wanted absolutely no part of him. It had tickled him to no end. His interest in her had been snagged simply because it had been so long since a woman had been so blatantly rude or downright cold toward him. Usually they were falling all over themselves trying to impress him. And he wasn't easily impressed.

But judging from Cassie's cold response to him, if he didn't know better, he'd think he was losing his touch.

"I do appreciate everything you've done," Cassie finally said, as she glanced toward the back of the shop for Sofie. "I don't know what brought this on. Sofie's been doing well in school. She's been making friends and getting along with all the other kids so I don't know when or how this started. More importantly, I'm not sure I know how to handle it," she admitted honestly, feeling grossly incompetent all of a sudden. "Sofie's always gotten along so well with everyone. And she's certainly never been teased before."

"This isn't Sofie's fault, and I don't think this teasing has gone on much beyond today," he said, trying to reassure her. "The school is far too aware of teasing and bullying to let something like this go on for very long. I've spent the past five years or so working with school officials to develop a strict no-tolerance policy for bullying in order to make the school a place where every child feels safe and comfortable, and is praised for their individual talents, not ridiculed." He sighed. "But once in a while, kids will be kids and something like this happens. The kids forget or someone is feeling hurt or inferior or disconnected from their parents, and teasing and bullying can be the result."

"Do you think that's what happened?" It sounded a lot less dramatic than she'd originally envisioned. "I mean, the idea of my daughter being bullied or teased at school is not a pleasant thought."

"I know, Cassie," he said quietly, sincerity shining in his eyes. "And I'm really sorry. But we know a lot more about this now than we ever did before and I'm certain with a little help from all of us Sofie will be able to handle this situation and be just fine." He hesitated, meeting her gaze. "That is, if you'll let me help?"

"Let you?" Shaking her head, she laughed, but the sound held no humor. "I'd be grateful for anything you can do or suggest." When it came to her daughter or her daughter's welfare, Cassie had no pride. She'd do anything and everything she could to keep her daughter happy, safe and secure, and if that meant dancing with a devil, well, all someone had to do was play the right music and show her the proper steps.

Giving another quick glance toward the back, wanting to make certain Sofie wasn't within earshot, Cassie shoved back her dark hair with a shaky hand. "I don't want my daughter thinking that the solution to any problem is running away."

"No, of course not," Beau said. "One of the most effective tools we can use right now to help Sofie through this is something we call the three C's." He smiled at her look of confusion. "It stands for caring, cooperation and conflict resolution. The caring obviously comes from you and all the adults in Sofie's life. She needs to know that you understand this is a difficult time for her, and that she should feel free to tell you when anything has upset her, especially at school."

"That's fine from my end, but where does the cooperation come in?" Cassie asked, crossing her arms, simply to hide her nervousness. "How do we go about getting the cooperation of the kids who are teasing her?" Thrashing them probably wasn't a viable option even if it did sound appealing at the moment.

"Why don't you let me work with Sofie on that?" he asked, and she hesitated, but finally nodded. Beau was thoughtful for a moment. "Generally, Cassie, when a child is teasing or bullying someone else, it stems from their own lack of self-esteem or their own feelings of inferiority. Or perhaps it has to do with an emotional crisis they're going through. A divorce, a death, any number of things can trigger these feelings in kids, especially when there's a decided disconnect between the child and his or her parents. If a child feels powerless in a situation, then he tends to gravitate toward behavior that will make him or her feel powerful."

"Teasing and bullying?" Cassie asked, suddenly understanding, and he nodded.

"Exactly. Sofie's new at school and the science fair is really a big deal here. Maybe someone felt a bit intimidated by Sofie's knowledge, maybe they were afraid she might have a better project or show them up. As a result, they began teasing her."

"And teasing her shakes her confidence and her self-esteem," Cassie said with a nod as things grew clearer. "And makes them feel better about themselves?"

"Exactly. Maybe that wasn't the original intention, but it is the result."

"I just don't want her to be hurt," she said softly, blinking away a surprising flash of tears.

"Cassie." Beau laid his hand on her shoulder and her gaze flew to his. She hadn't known he'd crossed the room and was standing so close to her. Her heart began doing a wicked two-step. He was so close she could smell his scent. Warm, woodsy, masculine and very appealing. She tried not to scowl.

"I promise you we can fix this, and fix it in such a way as to have as little damage emotionally, physically or psychologically to Sofie as possible," he said, giving her shoulder a gentle squeeze of encouragement. "But, you're going to have to trust me," he added quietly.

"Trust *you?*" She hadn't trusted a man in a long time and the idea of trusting a man when it came to her *daughter,* well, that idea was outright foreign to her. She didn't trust any man *that* much.

Besides, how was she supposed to trust the man when she wasn't comfortable standing in the same room with him?

Cassie took a deep breath and forced herself to meet Beau's gaze. She didn't have much choice in the matter, she realized. If she wanted to help her daughter, if she wanted her daughter to learn how to deal with life's problems and not think running from them was the answer, she was going to need his help.

And that apparently meant trusting him. At least in this limited capacity. If only for Sofie's sake.

But that didn't mean she had to like it!

"Okay. Fine," she said abruptly, taking a step away from him to turn and busily fold Sofie's coat and winter garments. "Do you have a lot of experience with this teasing stuff?" she asked, glancing up at him nervously.

"Actually, I do," he said. "As I mentioned I've been working with the schools to develop an anti-teasing and anti-bullying campaign. And," he added with a sigh, "I had my fair share of teasing when I was in school as well," he admitted. "Which is what started my interest in this subject and kids to begin with." He paused for a moment and she watched something dark and unfathomable move into his eyes. "Growing up, there were times I was teased unmercifully. Running away would have been a great option if only I'd thought of it," he admitted with a self-deprecating chuckle that actually made her smile. "So I know how Sofie feels. It's hard to be the smartest kid in school, and it's hard when you're the object of teasing. Which is why it was so important for me to start this program at the schools in the first place." He shrugged. "Like I said, it's been working pretty well, but once in a while…" His voice trailed off as his gaze met hers. Cassie merely stared at him, trying to absorb everything he was telling her.

"*You* were teased?" she repeated in surprise, then she chuckled. "I can't imagine anyone teasing you. For what? Being too perfect?" The moment the words were out, she flushed, realizing what she'd said, but he merely smiled. It warmed his eyes, chasing away the darkness, and softening his entire face.

"Uh, actually, I was teased because I was too smart, and because I was overweight and wore glasses. And to add insult to injury, everyone else had parents and I just had my uncle, Jasper—who everyone in town considers rather eccentric."

"I'm so sorry," Cassie said, hearing the pain from his youth still radiating in his voice. "But eccentric is a relative term around here. My mother's the town psychic, remember? And my aunt Louella is the town astrologer. So you have to go pretty far and wide to convince me someone else is eccentric," she finished with a laugh.

Together, her mother and aunt could easily qualify as the town's certifiable eccentrics.

"I guarantee Uncle Jasper definitely qualifies as eccentric as well," Beau admitted with a chuckle. "And he's also an amateur astronomer. Sofie told me she's very interested in the solar system and the stars and planets."

"Yes, she is. In Madison, our next-door neighbor was a retired professor and an amateur astronomer. She would invite Sofie over and show her how to look through her telescope, explaining everything Sofie saw. She's the one who got Sofie interested in science and astronomy and the solar system to begin with."

"Well, we actually have an observatory on our property."

"You're kidding?" The rambling old house on the edge of town had been little more than a curiosity piece—fodder for gossip for years. It was hard to believe that there was actually an observatory on the grounds. Or much else.

"Nope. Not kidding. In fact, I invited Sofie to dinner this evening so she could see for herself. I think we might be able to use Sofie's interest in science to help her with this teasing problem."

"Dinner?" Cassie repeated suspiciously and his eyes twinkled a moment before he threw back his head and laughed. "What," she demanded. "What on earth are you laughing at?"

"You," he said simply, stroking a finger down her cheek and almost making her jump out of her skin. He shook his head. "Cassie, I wish you didn't act like I'd just invited you to dinner in the devil's den," he teased, making her flush. "Most people in town think I'm a pretty upstanding citizen," he reminded her.

"Well, you said…dinner," she stammered and he nodded.

"That's right, I did." Casually, he slipped his hands in his coat pockets and rocked back on his heels. "But I was thinking more along the lines of chocolate, peanut-butter-and-banana sandwiches with milk, as opposed to say roses, candlelight and moonlight." He shrugged. "It's merely to help Sofie, Cass. Like I said, she's going to need our help if she's going to conquer this problem." He cocked his head and looked at her. "So what do you say? Do you think you can give me the benefit of the doubt and have dinner at my house tonight? For Sofie's sake, of course," he added with a twinkle in his eye that only made her more suspicious.

"Just dinner?" she clarified and he nodded, raising his hand in the air as if taking an oath.

"Just dinner. Promise."

Cassie rubbed her chilled arms. "Fine," she all but snapped. "Dinner it is then."

He glanced at his watch. "I've got to run, but I'll see you both around…six?"

"Fine." Having dinner with the town Romeo wasn't nearly as bad as having her daughter's feelings hurt so bad that she was contemplating running away.

Cassie glanced at Beau one last time before he headed out the door and her traitorous heart flipped over and fluttered, annoying her to no end.

She could handle this. And him, she told herself.

She hoped!

Chapter Two

By the time Cassie closed the salon for the night she was late. A last-minute walk-in had delayed her by almost an hour and a half.

It was dark now, and the weather had turned bitter and nasty. Snow was falling much harder, slicking the streets and coating the sidewalks, making both walking and driving hazardous. Luckily, she didn't have too far to go, and Beau had picked up Sofie earlier because Cassie was running so late.

Cassie shut off the lights for the night, grabbed her purse and let herself out the front door, locking up behind her.

Standing on the sidewalk, blanketed by fast-falling snow, she couldn't help but grin when she looked at the front of her shop, feeling an unexpected thrill.

She'd done it, she thought giddily, resisting the urge to hug herself as she headed toward her car. It had taken her six long, hard years to accomplish her dreams, she thought with a sigh as she brushed snow off her windshield, then unlocked the car and got in. But it had been worth it. Every terrifying moment. Safety and security for herself and her daughter, as well as her own hard-won independence, were what were important to her, what she'd worked so hard to gain.

While other women her age were living a carefree existence, out shopping for shoes, sipping lattes and partying at night while they patiently waited for Mr. Right to show up, she was struggling to put food on the table and keep a roof over their heads.

She'd learned firsthand how high the cost of trusting the wrong man could be. And she was determined not to make that kind of mistake—with *any* man—ever again.

Which was why Dr. Beau Bradford frightened her so much, she realized with a shiver. He reminded her far too much of Sofie's selfish, irresponsible father. An immature young man who had used his good looks and charm to infiltrate her young life and take advantage of her inexperience and her youth. Then just as quickly he had used his parents' money and power to extricate himself from her life once he'd learned they were going to be teenage parents.

In spite of all the hardships she'd endured in order to keep and raise her daughter, Cassie had never regretted her decision to become a single parent, not for one moment, because Sofie was worth more than life itself.

And things had been going fairly well until about a month ago, when a trip home to Cooper's Cove for her aunt Louella's wedding had changed their lives.

Trixie, the owner of the town beauty salon, had said she was retiring and looking for someone to take over the running and managing of the shop—someone who'd also be interested in buying it.

Afraid to get her hopes up, Cassie had spent three days negotiating with Trixie. On the third day, she'd finally signed the papers agreeing to manage the shop for five years with a percentage of the monthly profits going toward a buy-out. Within a week, she'd secured financing for a small-business loan to remodel and update the shop. And she was on her way. In five years the shop would be hers and hers alone. Bought and paid for with her own hands and hard work, she thought now, squinting to see through her snow-covered windshield as she slowly inched down Main Street.

She'd also accepted her mother's offer to move back home. Now that Aunt Louella had married and moved out, her mother had been living all alone in that big house. Cassie had to admit that her mom wasn't getting any younger and she worried about her being alone.

Cassie sighed again as she squinted harder in the darkness, trying to find the turnoff to Beau's house.

Beau's towering, crumbling house finally came into view, and Cassie let out a shaky breath as she slowly turned into the long driveway. She hated driving in the snow and ice, especially when it was so dark and cold.

The three-story stone house with the wide, straight driveway sat back at least a half mile from the road, making it difficult to see clearly through the snowy windshield. Snow was falling so hard now that visibility was nearly nil.

Lights were blazing inside and out and Cassie had to smile as she turned off her car. The house looked like one of those spooky old mansions in the campy horror flicks she used to love as a teen.

Grabbing her purse and gloves from the seat, she opened her car door, and braced herself for the cold and windy walk to the huge front door. Huddling inside her coat and clutching her purse to her chest, she stood on the front stoop for a few seconds, admiring the beautiful classic lines of the old stone house. It must have been a showplace at one time.

There was an old silver knocker on the door, but no bell, so she lifted the knocker and heard the resounding boom inside. She waited a moment, expecting Dr. Beau to open the door. But when it was slowly pulled open with a creak, Cassie found herself peering into the eyes of a small, rotund man who strongly resembled a mischievous leprechaun.

"Aye, who is it bothering me now?" he bellowed, his voice tinged with a heavy Irish brogue. Scowling, he blinked at her from around the door as if she'd materialized out of thin air.

Cassie swallowed, resisting the urge to step back. She had a feeling this was Dr. Beau's uncle.

He was about as round as he was tall. His white fringe of hair sprouted in tufts around his ears and temples as if he'd been tugging at it. His eyes were big, blue and twinkling with good humor, but at the moment, they were also a bit confused, as if she'd interrupted him from some intense project. His cheeks were full and rosy, as if he'd been dashing about in the snow.

He looked like a slightly unkempt *mad scientist* leprechaun. Cassie resisted the urge to chuckle. Now she knew what Beau had meant about his uncle being…eccentric. In spite of it, she had to admit he was absolutely adorable.

"Have you found them, yet?" he asked in a conspiratorial whisper, surprising her as he intently peered around the door at her.

"Found them?" Cassie repeated, blinking back at him.

He nodded. "Aye, lassie, I'm heartily afraid they've gone off on their own again." He looked at her, eyes wide and innocent. "Oh, don't be alarmed, it's not the first time, lassie, no siree. They've conspired for years to drive me daft. And now, I'm afraid they've gone off on their own again. Sprouted legs as sure as I'm standing here."

"Sprouted legs?" Cassie repeated. She leaned closer to him. "Who?" she whispered, glancing around to see if someone sprouting legs was in the vicinity.

"Me spectacles, of course, lassie," he admitted with a sad shake of his head. "They've gone a'traveling again," he added with another sigh, and a light, impatient tug on his white hair, making Cassie smile again. "They're trying to drive me daft for sure."

"Um…actually," she began slowly, as she reached toward him. "Um, may I?"

His face was blank as he blinked up at her. "Aye, yes, please, please," he encouraged with a wave, letting his gaze follow her hands so that his eyes nearly rolled back in his head.

"I think this should do it," Cassie said, lowering his glasses from where they'd been hiding on his balding head to rest them gently on his nose.

He blinked owlishly at her from behind the thick, heavy glasses as if seeing clearly for the first time in a long time. Then his face cleared and he beamed at her.

"Ah, so that's where they went off to," he said. "I've been searching for them for hours." Now that he had his glasses on, he looked her over from head to toe. "Well, for

St. Margaret's sake, lassie, who on earth left you standing out in the snow and cold?" he asked as if there was someone else in the foyer deliberately being rude to her. "Come in, come in. 'Tis colder than an Englishman's heart out there," he said with a cluck of his tongue, reaching for her hands and drawing her into the warmth of the huge foyer. "Ah, lass, I'm sorry, you'll think I've no manners now that you're chilled to the bone."

Cassie shivered a bit as she stepped inside and snuck a quick glance at the interior. She almost caught her breath. The foyer was as wide as her mother's living room and twice as long, with black-and-white marble tile floors, peeling wallpaper, and a gorgeous, but delicate fading fresco on the ceiling. There were two large, elegant arched entryways on either side of the foyer, leading to what she assumed were other rooms.

"Uncle Jasper?" Beau walked into the foyer from one of the adjoining rooms, one hand in Sofie's. The moment he spotted Cassie, he stopped dead in his tracks, his eyes meeting hers. She had to swallow hard, knowing that intense masculine gaze was taking in every inch of her.

"You made it." His smile was wide and welcoming, as his gaze slid over her and a pool of warmth puddled in her center.

Lord, the man's impact was incredible. No wonder every woman in town was after him.

"Mama!" Sofie skipped toward her, delight shining in her eyes. "Guess what? Guess what?" Hair a mess, Sofie was all but bouncing out of her scuffed and bruised school shoes. "Dr. Beau and I already looked at the stars and the solar system and Dr. Beau's gonna help me with my science project."

"He is, is he?" Cassie said, grinning down at her daughter. A fierce surge of love rose up in her. "That's wonderful, honey." Absently, Cassie reached out and tightened one of Sofie's barrettes so her hair wouldn't fall in her face.

Sofie tugged her mother's hand. "And you know what else, Mama? Uncle Jasper's got a telescope, a real big one and he said after dinner I could look through it, and maybe I could see to another planet! And then, Mama, we're gonna play checkers. Me and Uncle Jasper." Sofie tugged on her hand again. "And Dr. Beau says he has lots of good ideas for my science fair project," Sofie continued, obviously thrilled as she turned to stare adoringly at Beau. "And he said…that maybe…" Sofie hesitated, frowning back up at her mother.

"What, sweetheart?" Cassie asked, bending down so she was eye level with her daughter.

"Well, do you think maybe…I mean…could I maybe invite some kids from school over to help with my science project?" Sofie peeked at her mother from under lowered lashes.

"You want to invite some kids from school over, honey?" Cassie repeated in surprise and her daughter nodded, then grinned, rocking back and forth on the heels of her school shoes.

"Dr. Beau said sometimes it's good to have the help of your friends with a big project. 'Specially a big science project."

"He did, did he?" Cassie said, glancing up at Beau. That was some miracle act the man had performed, Cassie realized, wondering just what he'd said to her daughter. This afternoon Sofie had wanted to run away from the very same kids she now wanted to invite over.

She was definitely going to have to learn the man's secret.

"Well, I think it would be wonderful to invite your friends over. How about on Sunday? The shop is closed and I'll be home all day, and I can make my special homemade pizzas." She brushed Sofie's dark hair from her eyes. "What do you say?"

"Really?" Sofie breathed, her eyes going wide in excitement. "Mama makes the bestest pizzas ever."

"She does?" Beau said with a smile and a lift of his brow. His gaze remained on Cassie, making her want to fidget. She should probably invite him for pizza, she realized, considering how kind he'd been to Sofie. But she just couldn't get the words out, not wanting to willingly spend more time than necessary with the man. "I guess I'll have to try some."

"Wanna come for lunch Sunday?" Sofie asked and Cassie almost groaned.

Beau saw the look on her face before she could disguise it and his eyes twinkled mischievously. "I think that would be lovely, Sofie. Thank you." He merely flashed Cassie a grin as she scowled. He'd done that deliberately, she realized. Deliberately agreed to come to lunch simply because he knew he made her uncomfortable. The blasted man!

While Cassie and Beau merely stared at each other, Sofie tugged her mother's hand again. "And Mama, Uncle Jasper says I'm really, really smart, and that being smart is a good thing, and not any reason to run away. Isn't that right, Uncle Jasper?"

"Aye, absolutely, lassie, 'tis a truly wonderful thing," Jasper confirmed with a nod of his head, reaching for her free hand. "The very best thing," he added, taking Sofie's hand and giving Cassie and Beau an encompassing glance. "And now, if you'll excuse us, the littlest princess and I have a date." He winked at Sofie, who beamed at him, clearly delighted to be the center of attention. "Isn't that right, lassie?"

Sofie's dark head bobbed. "That's right, Uncle Jasper."

Uncle Jasper's voice trailed off as he led Sofie out of the foyer. Cassie couldn't help it, she started to laugh.

"I'm sorry," she said to Beau, trying to contain herself. "But he's absolutely…adorable." Still laughing, she shook her head. "And totally charming. He's just wonderful."

"Yeah, he is," Beau said as he glanced after his uncle. "The best thing that ever happened to me," he added softly, and Cassie was surprised by the genuine emotion in his voice.

"He raised you, didn't he?" she asked gently, remembering what he'd said this afternoon about being teased, and Beau nodded.

"I was five when my parents were killed in a car accident on the way home from a scientific seminar. All I knew was that my parents went away for the weekend and never came back."

"I'm so sorry," Cassie said, her heart aching for him. She could still hear the shock and pain of the enormous loss somewhere in the deep timbre of his voice. Unconsciously, she reached out and laid a hand on his arm, instinctively wanting to comfort. She couldn't imagine what it would have been like to have been orphaned at such a young age.

"My uncle Jasper was my father's only brother, and the brilliant eccentric in the family, according to my dad, who was no slouch in either department himself. I'd never met Uncle Jasper, at least not that I remembered." He laughed suddenly, dragging a hand through his black hair. "So here I was, sitting at the bottom of the steps in this big old house—my parents' house," he clarified, glancing around the familiar foyer. "Which wasn't much different from this place. I'm all alone in the world, and scared out of my mind when the front door bursts open and this ball of Irish energy comes bounding in. I could only stare at him with my mouth open," he recalled, humor glinting in his eyes. "He had on a shirt that was buttoned crookedly and hanging out of pants which weren't zipped, but were held up by some kind of metal chain he'd somehow gotten tangled and knotted around him. He had on two pairs of glasses, one pair on his eyes, one pair resting on top of his head, and a pair of mismatched shoes." Beau chuckled. "Actually, it was a slipper and a shoe. He usually gets distracted halfway through getting dressed so that's why he's only half-dressed most of the time. Either Shorty or I usually catch up to him to fix him up before he goes out in public, but I didn't know that then. Then, I was just a scared, bewildered five-year-old," he admitted quietly. "Especially when the first words out of Uncle Jasper's mouth were 'Can you cook, laddie?'" He did a fantastic imitation of his uncle's heavy Irish brogue and Cassie covered her mouth to smother a chuckle, visualizing the picture.

"And what did you say?"

Tongue in cheek, he shook his head. "The truth. I said very solemnly, 'I'm sorry, sir, but I'm only five years old.'"

Cassie's tender heart almost melted. She could almost see him, she realized. The small, scared vulnerable little boy, all alone in the world, not knowing what was to become of him, facing Uncle Jasper for the first time.

She thought of her own daughter at that age, how totally

vulnerable she'd been, and Cassie's heart ached a little more for him.

"Uncle Jasper just nodded, then he took one good long look at me, went down on his knee so we were eye level, opened his arms and said, 'Aye laddie, I'm sorry this happened to us, but I've been waiting my whole life for you.' One single tear slowly ran down his face and I knew then Uncle Jasper was probably just as scared as I was. He just hugged me tight and said, 'Me and Shorty, we came to take you home, laddie.'" Beau's voice had dropped, but now he chuckled again, then shook his head. "And I knew everything was going to be okay," he said with a careless shrug that she knew hid a well of emotion. "We've been together and a family ever since."

"That's a wonderful story," she said quietly, blinking the mist from her eyes. "Did you ever learn to cook?" she asked, making him chuckle again.

"Nope, can't even boil eggs," Beau said with a grin, closing the distance between them to help her off with her coat. He leaned close until his breath warmed the back of her neck, making her vividly aware of the pulsing ache of yearning slowly spreading its hot fingers through her belly. Cassie had to swallow to dispel some of her nervousness, smothering the wave of awareness that was making every female nerve ending stand at attention.

She was supposed to be immune to this type of man, she reminded herself firmly.

"Cassie," he whispered close to her ear. "I want you to know I feel exactly the same way about your mother and your aunt as you do about Uncle Jasper," he said, looping her coat over his arm and stepping back from her. "They're wonderful as far as I'm concerned."

"Well, thank you, but I'm going to remind you of that the next time mama or Aunt Louella rushes into your office and tells you to do some outrageous thing like turn all your faucets on so that your pipes don't freeze when it's not even cold out."

Beau chuckled. "Sounds like you've had plenty of experience with the outrageous?"

"Living with Mama and Aunt Louella was always one outrageous adventure after another," she admitted. "But I adore both of them and wouldn't have it any other way."

He chuckled again, then grew sober, his gaze finding hers and sending a fluttering straight through to her timid heart. "I'm glad you made it," he said softly. "It's a miserable night."

She wanted to glance away, to break contact with those gorgeous blue eyes, but mentally scolded herself for being a coward.

He was just a man, for goodness sake. She'd dealt with hundreds of men in her life, probably thousands. There was certainly no reason to get all flustered every time this one looked at her.

Still, there was something very different about this man that made her very aware of her own feelings and emotions. It was just a tad unnerving since she truly thought herself immune to *any* kind of man.

She rubbed her hands together and glanced back at the windows on either side of the large front door, wanting to break the connection between them.

"It is getting bad out," she admitted with a rueful smile. "I could barely see driving here because the snow's coming down so hard. And I don't even want to think about having to drive home in it."

"Don't worry about it," he said, taking her arm and leading her out of the foyer. "I've got a heavy four-wheel-drive vehicle so I can make house calls no matter what the weather. If it gets much worse I'll drive you and Sofie home, and Shorty can return your car in the morning. Deal?"

She looked into his eyes and had to remind herself she was merely here to help her daughter. She was doing this for Sofie. There was nothing between *them*. Nothing personal at all, she reminded herself. So all these feelings coursing through her, confusing her, alarming her, were to be ignored.

"Deal," she agreed reluctantly, making him smile.

"When I picked Sofie up from your mother's, we had a chance to chat," he said with a mysterious smile, glancing down at her as he led the way through the foyer. "And before I picked up Sofie, I made a couple of other stops at a couple of other first graders' house's as well," he said with a knowing lift of his brow. "Seems there is a bit of disruption going on with two of the boys. One's parents are separating—"

"Oh, I'm sorry," Cassie said softly.

"And the other's grandmother recently passed away very suddenly. They were apparently very close so the boy's quite traumatized by the loss."

"Oh, Beau, the poor thing," Cassie said, her heart softening toward the boys whom just this afternoon she wanted to thrash. "So they're both having some personal problems of their own. I guess their behavior is understandable under the circumstances."

"Understandable, yes, but certainly not justifiable, Cassie," he said quietly. "Just because they're having personal problems doesn't give them the right to take out their pain on someone else."

"You're right," she said, rubbing her hands up and down her arms. "But at least we know there is a reason for this behavior and they're not just being cruel to Sofie."

He chuckled. "It would be hard to find anyone who's deliberately cruel in Cooper's Cove. I think the mayor forbade it decades ago. But it does explain what I was trying to tell you this afternoon, those feelings of insecurity I was talking about."

Cassie nodded, listening intently as he continued.

"So, I had a little chat with both boys, and then with their parents. Separately of course, which is how I found out all this info. And I think I've worked up a solution for all involved, at least to the teasing and bullying problem." A shadow passed over his features. "Let's hope it's enough to do the trick."

She was desperately trying to pay attention to his words, but he was so close she could see the sparkle in his eyes and the small laugh lines around his mouth….

He'd changed into more casual clothes, she suddenly realized. Gone was the professional suit he'd always worn in his office. Now, he had on soft, well-worn jeans, a heavy Irish cable knit sweater and work boots. Much to Cassie's annoyance it made him look far less intimidating and a great deal more appealing.

She forced herself to keep her mind on the subject at hand. "Judging from the change in Sofie's attitude since you brought her home from school this afternoon, she's feeling better about the situation as well," Cassie said, still shocked by the difference in her daughter. This problem with Sofie hadn't been far from her mind all afternoon. "It's amazing, isn't it? How quickly their emotions change?"

"With kids this age, it really is just a lot of confidence," he admitted as he pulled open a closet door in the expansive foyer and hung up her coat. "So much of their emotions and attitudes are fed by their immediate world. Parents, family and friends make up everything, and are everything to them, and as long as everything is copacetic with all three, they're happy." He shrugged. "But when they're not, that's when problems develop."

"And you think that's what's happened here?" she asked, and he nodded.

"Yes, I'm afraid that's exactly what happened. But I've talked with the boys, and with Sofie, so now let's see if we can work out some kind of truce to keep them all happy. Are you hungry?" he asked abruptly and she paled a bit.

"I'm…uh…fine," she said, avoiding his gaze and placing a hand on her growling stomach. He watched her carefully, then tried to smother a chuckle. "What?" she demanded. "What on earth are you laughing about now?" It was as if he could read her mind and it was unnerving.

"You," he said. "And the look on your face when I asked you if you were hungry." His eyes gleamed. "Let me guess, the prospect of a chocolate, peanut butter and banana sandwich is not exactly at the top of your dinner choices, am I right?" he asked with a lift of his brow.

"You're right," she admitted with a laugh and rueful shake of her head.

"Well, don't worry about it. I told Shorty we were having guests for dinner and he almost blistered my ears when I told him what I wanted to serve." He held out his hand to her. "So he's prepared Sofie her favorite sandwiches and something a bit more adult for us. Shall we?"

She looked at his outstretched hand as if it were a snake

about to strike. She honestly couldn't remember the last time she was so skittish around a man. But then again, she couldn't remember the last time she was this close to a man. Her experience with Sofie's father had left a bitter taste in her mouth and scared her off all men. As far as she was concerned, she couldn't trust her own judgment, not when it came to men, so she simply kept her distance.

Besides, she was far too busy trying to support herself and her daughter to worry about impressing some man or squeezing time out of her hectic life to accommodate him. There had always seemed so many more important things to do.

But now, with Beau, Cassie simply couldn't fall back on her usual routine of indifference and disdain. Like it or not, she *needed* his help and so did her daughter. So she was going to curb her own feelings and put Sofie's needs ahead of her own. Again. It was something that had become second nature to her from the moment of her beloved daughter's birth.

I'm doing this for Sofie, she mentally reminded herself and immediately felt a bit better. But she'd feel a *lot* better if Beau Bradford looked less like a movie star and more like a toad.

"Shall we?" he repeated, still holding out his hand to her, as if daring her to take it.

Cassie pressed her free hand to her shaky tummy as she let him escort her out of the foyer, reminding herself once again she wasn't the least bit interested in him—personally.

Her obligation was to Sofie and Sofie's welfare. Sofie's health, heart and happiness came first in Cassie's life, and she wasn't about to jeopardize any of them because of one gorgeous man. No matter how charming he was.

Chapter Three

"Oh my word!" Cassie said, coming to a dead halt in the room Beau had referred to as the atrium. She spun in a circle, trying to take in everything. "This is…magnificent," she breathed, stunned by the sheer size and beauty of the room.

Floor-to-ceiling windows, left uncovered to allow full access to Mother Nature's beauty, served as three of the room's walls, allowing a breathtaking view of the landscape as far as the eye could see.

Lights and stars twinkled against the inky blackness, and the flakes of fast-falling snow sparkled like glittering diamonds floating toward earth. It was a scene out of a beautiful, romantic movie.

A roaring fire in the huge fireplace at one end of the room provided both light and a warm, homey coziness that instantly wrapped around you in welcome.

The floors were a beautiful aged wood and the colorful, if faded, Persian carpets that dotted the floor served merely to highlight the gorgeous grain and surrounding patina. On either side of the enormous, roaring fireplace were custom-made oak bookshelves filled with more books than Cassie had ever seen outside of a public library.

Nestled in one corner, right in front of the beautiful view, was a small, elegant table set for two. An eggshell tablecloth of what looked like beautiful aged silk adorned the small, round dinner table. Fresh flowers sparkled in a shimmering crystal vase. White taper candles were perched elegantly in a small rosette of expensive-looking crystal, just waiting to be lit.

Cassie selfconsciously glanced down at herself and felt just a tad out of place in her stained salon uniform and work shoes. She wasn't accustomed to dining at tables adorned with silk linens and candles nestled in crystal.

Feeling more than a little off balance now, Cassie tried to ignore how romantic the scene looked to her, and kept her gaze moving.

This wasn't personal, she told herself. The table was probably always set in that corner like that. It wasn't any big deal just because she was there.

But whether or not it was, she caught herself sneaking appreciative glances back at the table simply because it looked so breathtaking against the dark glittering backdrop Mother Nature had provided.

"This is the most incredible room I've ever seen." Fascinated, Cassie merely roamed for a moment, soaking in the beauty of everything, nearly overwhelmed by the aged opulence reflected in every single antique knickknack and furnishing in the room.

She had no idea what it would have been like to grow up surrounded by this kind of luxury or beauty. It was a bit faded now, yes, but the wealth it took to put together a house like this still shone through. She couldn't help but feel just a wee bit intimidated. It was the same way she'd felt the one and only time she'd been in Sofie's father's opulent childhood home.

Trying to banish that memory, Cassie allowed herself the pleasure of just taking everything in. She walked to the front of the fireplace, stunned by the amount of heat generated from such an enormous hearth. It was so large an adult could easily have stood up in it.

Over the intricately carved oak mantel was a large oil painting of a rather gruff-looking man who had the same mischievous twinkle in his eyes as Beau and his uncle. His white hair tufted out around his temples and ears much the same way as Uncle Jasper's did.

"Family trait," Beau said from behind her, startling her again so that she jumped. He laid a hand on her shoulder. "Cassie, you're going to have to stop doing that."

"Doing what?" she asked, rubbing her hands up and down her arms, vividly aware of how close he was to her and how her traitorous body responded every time he touched her.

"Jumping every time I come near you," he said quietly, taking her by the shoulders and gently turning her to face him. "Cassie." His gaze scanned her face and she sensed that he could see the fear and vulnerability in her eyes. Tenderly, he squeezed her shoulders. "I don't know what on earth you've heard about me, but clearly it must be something pretty awful to make you nearly jump out of your shoes every time I come near you."

"No, it's…not that," she lied, and he smiled.

"Cassie. I know how people talk. They've gossiped about

me my whole life. And I know what they say," he added softly, making her heart ache for the pain that knowledge had to bring. "Remember, I grew up here, just like you, and I know how the gossip vines work. But I would think you'd be the last person in the world to believe gossip."

He had her there. And had managed to make her feel small and ridiculous simply because he was absolutely right. She had grown up amid gossip and she *knew* better. And yet, she'd allowed herself to judge him simply from things she'd heard about him, not from her own experiences.

And just that afternoon hadn't the kids made assumptions about Sofie without really knowing the truth, assumptions that had hurt the young child's feelings? How on earth could Cassie do the same to the man who'd promised to help her daughter?

She couldn't, she realized—not in good conscience. Or she would be just as wrong as the kids at school had been today.

"Cassie, I'm sure you've heard some wild stories about me and women, but all I ask is that before you make up your mind about me, you judge me for yourself, by your own experiences and not by rumors or innuendo." Watching her carefully, Beau gently lifted her chin. "Do you think you can do that?"

She forced herself to meet his gaze, to look into his eyes and see the emotions swirling there. And she remembered all the rumors she'd heard about his womanizing. She wasn't entirely sure now how true or accurate they'd been, and it shamed her to think she might have misjudged him just as her own daughter had been misjudged.

"Yes. Yes, of course," she assured him.

She dared to glance up at him again and her mouth went dry when she looked at his mouth. Oh, Lord, that mouth. It looked soft and warm and very…talented. That was the only word she could think of.

He was standing directly in front of her, closer than any man had been in a very long time. So close she could feel the warmth of his body heat, smell the scent that danced along his skin. It was such a mesmerizing, masculine scent it was almost dizzying. She had a sudden urge to stand on tiptoe and bury her face in his neck, to simply inhale that incredibly wonderful maleness.

Then there were his eyes, she thought dreamily. Gorgeous and blue, they reflected so many things, she realized now. Emotions she'd not thought him capable of simply because she'd prejudged and perhaps misjudged him based rumor and gossip.

Guilt landed like a hammer and Cassie realized just how unfair she'd been to Beau. He had been nothing but kind to her and her daughter. *Especially her daughter*. And for that alone he deserved her thanks, her gratitude and more importantly, he deserved to be treated fairly and with respect. She made a silent vow to do better; to *be* better and more fair. And most importantly, to give him a chance without any preconceived notions on her part.

"Dr. Bradford—"

"Beau," he corrected with a smile. "Only my patients call me Dr. Bradford and you're too old to be one of my patients."

"Beau," she conceded with a nod and a smile, laying her hands on his chest, surprised by how solid he was. "I'm sorry. Truly I am." Shaking her head, she licked her dry lips, embarrassed by her own behavior. She tried to gather her thoughts, but it wasn't easy when he was so close and his mouth, that wonderful, incredible mouth, was just inches away.

"It's not you," she finally managed to get out. "Truly, Beau. It's me. I haven't been around a man in a very long time," she admitted, feeling her cheeks flush at the admission. "I'm not used to having one help my daughter. And…it's just everything that happened today sort of threw me for a loop," she managed to finish, knowing if she didn't step back from him, put some distance between them, she might do something she would regret.

"That's perfectly understandable," he said, stroking a thumb across her cheek and distracting her so much by his touch she forgot to step back.

"And I'm… I'm…so used to handling anything and everything on my own—"

"Without any help?" he said knowingly, and she nodded.

"Right. Without any help, especially *male* help. Maybe I've forgotten how to graciously accept help when it's needed." She could feel a flush warm her cheeks simply because it was the truth. Her natural reticence with men had led her to be downright rude to him, and that wasn't her way. She would never hurt someone's feelings or be deliberately rude to them. She had just let her own fears overwhelm her manners.

His brows drew together a bit. "Are you concerned about being indebted to me? Or concerned that perhaps I don't have Sofie's best interests at heart?"

"Oh, no, of course not," she said quickly, shaking her head. "It's just, Sofie and I have always been…well… we've always been alone, ever since she was born. We've always been a team, a two-woman team," she clarified.

"I've never had to reach out to a stranger for help before." She'd never before *allowed* herself to do that. But for her precious daughter, she'd do anything. "And it's not such an easy thing for me to do."

"Which bothers you more?" he asked, cocking his head to study her. "Asking for the help? Or needing the help?"

She had to think about it for a moment. "Both, actually," she admitted with a wan smile. "I guess I've always thought and believed myself to be pretty self-sufficient."

He nodded. "I think it's hard for anyone to admit they need help with something, but it's not a crime. And I assure you again that I have only Sofie's best interests at heart." He raised his hand in the air as if taking an oath. "I assure you my intentions toward your daughter are truly honorable."

She had to laugh. He'd made a moment of discomfort more comfortable by allowing her to laugh at herself and him. "Thank you," she said, her smile warmer.

He tilted her chin again so she was forced to look at him. "And my intentions toward her mother are just as honorable," he added softly, studying her face. "It's the neighborly thing to do," he said with a shrug. "It's no big deal, at least not in Cooper's Cove. So maybe if you think of it that way it might help. It happens all the time—one neighbor helping another. No one gives it a second thought. I just happen to have the expertise that you need in this particular instance. And if I had a problem and you had the ability or expertise to help me—as a good neighbor— wouldn't you?"

"Of course," she said without thinking. "That's the whole point of living in a small town," she admitted. "Knowing you're not alone and can always depend on someone."

"Exactly. So try not to think about this as anything more than one neighbor helping another. And remember that you'd do the same for me, or anyone else with a problem, so it's really no big deal. Do you think you can do that?"

Beau searched Cassie's face again, waiting for her response. While he could appreciate her beauty, and her spirit, he couldn't and wouldn't allow any woman to touch his heart or his emotions. It wasn't that he didn't like women, on the contrary, he loved them, adored them, and found them interesting and fascinating. But a brief encounter in medical school, when he'd fallen head first in love with another student and later heard her bragging about bagging the Bradford heir, had taught him to be more than careful when it came to women. He'd been devastated to learn that his only appeal had apparently been his fortune. And he'd been dodging and weaving fortune hunters ever since, not to mention all the candidates his uncle had tried to recruit as mates for him over for years.

All that experience had made him wary and steadfastly mistrustful of women, knowing it wasn't *him,* but something else—generally his *fortune*—that truly interested them. And he didn't think he could ever trust a woman not to have dollar signs as an underlying ulterior motive to her feelings, no matter how much she pretended otherwise.

"Boss!" The deep, baritone voice bellowed into the room, loud enough to make the air all but vibrate. Cassie jumped, startled, and pressed a hand to her rampaging heart. *"Boss!"* A man about the size of a small sequoia stomped into the room and her mouth almost fell open. "We got trouble, Boss. Big trouble. Your uncle, aye, looks like he's at it again." Dressed in faded jeans that hugged legs the size of tree-trunks, and a sleeveless black T-shirt,

the giant's bare arms—the size of sewer pipes—had intricate tattoos written in another language up and down them. His shock of white hair looked like it had been buzz cut with a lawn mower and each ear was adorned with several gold hoop earrings. His ski-sized boots stomped across the room and Cassie could have sworn the wooden floor trembled. Cassie had heard rumors about this man, but it was the first time she'd seen him. Instinctively, she inched closer to Beau.

"What is it now, Shorty?" Beau asked with a sigh, and Shorty shook his head.

"'Nay, Boss, 'tis not an it, but a *who*," he all but snarled. Age and life had carved deep crevices and lines in his face. The long, white scar that bisected his right eyebrow only added to the roughness. "Her name is Cordelia Vanden-something and I just got off the phone with her."

"What does she want?" Beau asked and Shorty's features moved into what some would probably call a sneer of a smile.

"Aye, since she was trying to finagle your schedule from me, I imagine the lassie wants…*you*," Shorty finished with a widening grin, clearly enjoying himself.

"Me?" Barely suppressing a shudder, Beau gaped at him. "Oh Shorty, please no, not another one." He all but groaned. "Jasper promised."

"Aye, he surely did, Boss. And you know he means well, but the minute a thought or a promise enters your uncle's foggy brain, it sneaks out the other side just as fast, and more often than not, it's leaving nary a remembrance behind, either." Shorty shrugged massive shoulders.

"Excuse me?" Cassie said, looking from one man to the other, trying not to be thrown off base by how small the room suddenly seemed and how close Beau was. "Would someone mind telling me what's going on here?"

Beau and Shorty exchanged glances before Beau finally spoke. "It's a long story, Cassie, and, well—"

"Boss," Shorty said, interrupting him by placing a heavy hand on his shoulder. "You should let me do this. I can do it right quick now."

"Be my guest, then," Beau said with a smile.

"See," Shorty began, giving Cassie his attention, "Uncle Benny and the Boss's dad were the only two Bradford males, and since Uncle Jasper never married, the Doc here is the only Bradford heir left. So if the Doc doesn't make a match and have some wee ones, there ain't gonna be another Bradford heir. Ever." He gave the Doc a baleful look. "And," Shorty went on, "that means that Bradford Plastics might end up in…hostile hands, as it were. Not to mention not having a wee heir to carry on the Bradford name and legacy." Shorty hesitated for a moment, as if gathering his thoughts. "And Uncle Jasper has sort of decided that it's his job as Beau's…da…to find the right lassie for the Doc. And aye, if the truth be known, the Doc here ain't exactly getting any younger and he's not exactly been successful finding the right match on his own, either. A dismal failure if you want to know the truth," Shorty confided. "So Uncle Jasper decided to take matters into his own hands and step up the search."

"So Uncle Jasper's been matchmaking?" Cassie asked, her gaze going from Shorty to Beau, then back again.

"That's right," Shorty said, beaming at her and revealing a solid gold eyetooth. He gave Beau a wink and a hearty nudge. "Aye, this one's at least smart, Boss. Good-looking, too," he said, making Beau wince. Shorty leaned back to get a better vantage point to inspect her. "Looks like she's got a right fine pair of hips, Boss, more than ample for birthing babes as far as I can tell, so I don't see—"

"Shorty," Beau said, holding up his hand and trying to stop this train before it derailed and got them both mangled. "We can't just...*keep* Cassie—"

"And why the bloody hell not, Boss?" Shorty thundered, ham-sized hands on his hips. "I like *this* one," he said, sounding like a petulant teen. "She's smart and pretty. And she doesn't seem to be busy putting on airs like the others. And besides, she's already got experience with a wee one so we wouldn't have to do much training of her, either. So what's the problem? Why can't we keep her?" Shorty glared at Beau, crossing his arms across his chest as if the matter was now settled.

Cassie laughed, liking the man in spite of herself. "Uh...Shorty," she began, laying a hand on his arm. "I'm flattered you'd like to, uh, keep me, but I'm afraid I'm not in the market for a marriage partner. Or *any* partner," she clarified. "Sofie and I are a two-person team and I'm afraid all positions are currently filled."

Sighing, Shorty scratched his head and shrugged his massive shoulders as he glanced at Beau. "Aye, Boss, I tried. Truly I did."

"I know, and I appreciate it." Beau smiled. "So tell me what you said to this rude woman who called."

Shorty grinned, pleased with himself as he rocked back on his heels again. "Told her you were quarantined."

Beau's face went blank. "Excuse me?"

"Told the bloody rude woman that you were quarantined. Mumps," he added with another grin and a wink for Cassie. "Figured it would buy you some time."

Beau sighed. "Yes, better the whole town thinks the only pediatrician in town is quarantined with an infectious childhood disease than have one meddling fortune hunter searching for a marriageable husband for a young relative think that I'm not interested."

"Aye, see, we do think alike," Shorty said with another grin, ignoring Beau's pained look. "I figure you got two, maybe three days before you've got to hide like a river rat. But I done my part, you're on your own from here on out." Shorty sighed. "And now, it's time to get back to my kitchen." He glanced at the table he'd set earlier. "Better park yourselves since dinner will be ready shortly." He started to stomp back across the room, but stopped and turned back to Cassie. "And lassie, if you change your mind about letting us keep you, you'll let me know?"

"You'll be the first, Shorty." She grinned. "Promise."

"Aye. Appreciate it," he muttered, giving her a two-finger salute before stomping out of the room.

"Well," Beau said with a sigh as he led Cassie to the table. "That was interesting."

"Very," she said, trying to hide a laugh.

"Now you've met…my family." Beau sighed as he pulled out Cassie's chair. "My entire family." It was generally about this time a woman tried to drag him out the door since his family could hardly be considered normal or average, and not many women had the patience to put up with a house full of eccentrics. So Beau was a little surprised by Cassie's mild reaction.

"And you've met mine," Cassie said with a grin as she sat at the table. "But I've got to admit, for the first time in my life I think I've actually met someone who just might tie me for first place in the 'most eccentric family' contest."

Cassie unfolded her linen napkin and took a deep breath. "But Uncle Jasper and Shorty are still adorable," she added with a laugh. "And I can't wait to see how Mama and Uncle Jasper get along."

"Matchmaking, Cassie?" Beau asked with a grin and a lift of his brow as he pulled out his own chair and sat down.

"Me?" She flushed, then laughed. "Not on your life. I'm a firm believer in minding my own business, especially when it comes to matters of the heart."

"Sounds like a good practice to me," Beau admitted, unfolding his own napkin and smiling across the table at her. "Now if we could just convince our families of that."

"For someone who doesn't cook," Cassie commented less than an hour later as she finished the last of her filet and pushed her plate away, "I'll have to tell Shorty that was fabulous." She dabbed her mouth with her napkin.

"Shorty grills," Beau clarified, pushing his own plate away. "According to him there's a difference." He glanced across the table at her. The candlelight flickered over the elegant planes and angles of her face, making her look beautiful and ethereal. He couldn't remember when he'd enjoyed an evening more. "Thank you, Cassie, for tonight, for coming to dinner," he said. "And for trusting me enough to let me help Sofie."

"I think I'm the one who should be doing the thanking," she said, reaching for her crystal water glass. "For everything you've done." She hesitated, sipping her water. "You know it's hard to believe the change in Sofie just from this afternoon to when I got here this evening." She shook her head. "If I hadn't seen it with my own eyes, I don't know that I'd have believed it."

"Well, it's not totally over," he cautioned carefully, a slight frown on his face. "Let's just say we're at the beginning stages. I'm hoping now that I've talked to all the kids involved, and learned a little of the problems the boys are facing, the situation will be easier to deal with. Knowing you have a problem is the first step in solving it, especially with kids."

Fascinated, she leaned her chin on her hand and stared at him, mesmerized by the way the light played over his face. "How on earth did you learn so much about kids?" She laughed. "I mean, you don't have any, do you?" she asked abruptly, her gaze going to his. He shook his head.

"No. You heard Shorty attest to my lack of a 'wee heir.'" He shook his head. "I love kids, which is why I became a pediatrician, but having my own…" His voice trailed off and she could have sworn he'd shuddered. "Now that's another whole frightening ball of wax." He glanced down at his empty plate. He would never bring a child into the world unless it was into a happy and loving marriage. And since he had pretty much ruled out such a union, he had pretty much ruled out kids. Plus he knew too much about how blatantly cruel and selfish kids could be.

"Are you telling me you have a whole pediatric practice full of children, yet the idea of a child of your own *frightens* you?"

"Scares me spitless," he admitted with a nod and a sheepish smile.

"But why?"

"I guess this is a case of knowing too much for my own good. I know how many ways there are to screw up as a parent, I know how many ways a child can be terribly scarred just by the process of growing up, and I guess the idea of actually being responsible for the entire life of one small, vulnerable child is just terribly daunting to me," he admitted.

She nodded. "I understand that, actually." She laughed then, circling her finger around her water glass. "Luckily, at the time I got pregnant I was far too young and naive to even think about all the ways I could have screwed up. I guess it was a case of ignorance being truly bliss and I simply went with love and gut instinct."

"You've done a wonderful job with Sofie," he said quietly, his gaze meeting and holding hers. "She's a normal, healthy, well-adjusted little girl."

"When she's not intent on running away, you mean?" Cassie responded with a laugh, realizing she was enjoying herself. And him. It surprised her since she was a bit overwhelmed by what a gorgeous, available, interesting man he was.

"I think running away was simply a knee-jerk reaction, not something she really intended to do."

"Lord, I hope not." Cassie wanted to shudder.

He smiled. "I think she would have come home as soon as she had time to think about it. Or got scared. Whichever came first."

"Yeah, but luckily neither of those had to happen because you found her and were able to get her to talk to you, to tell you what the problem was."

"Sometimes the easiest thing for parents to do is simply *ask* their kids if there's anything wrong or if something is going on or bothering them."

"That's easy to say, but when you get caught up in the day-to-day business of life and parenting, sometimes we forget to do the simple things, like ask questions."

"In kids this age, asking them is the best way to gauge

their emotional temperature. If something's bothering them, or they're angry or upset, they'll simply tell you. *If you ask*," he added with a lift of his brow, then he shrugged. "Fortunately, at this age, kids are not old enough yet to disguise their feelings. It doesn't occur to them." He chuckled suddenly. "It's the teen years you have to really worry about."

This time she did groan. "Please, I was having such a good time."

"Were you?" he asked quietly, laying his hand over hers. Surprisingly she didn't jump this time.

"Yeah, actually, I was. I am," she said with a smile.

"Good. See, dinner with a neighbor can be pleasant and not the fear-inducing episode that all but terrorized you this afternoon."

Embarrassed a bit at how rude she'd been to him this afternoon in her shop, Cassie glanced out the window and sighed.

"You really have done a wonderful job with Sofie," he said softly, cupping her hand in his. "She's a bright, happy, very well-adjusted little girl with an insatiable curiosity to learn. Her desire for knowledge, to learn all that she can about everything around her, is really refreshing."

"You can blame me for that," she admitted. His hand was warm and gentle and oh so masculine, setting off sparks of intense desire and awareness somewhere deep inside her. "I guess I always felt inferior because I was never able to go to college like I planned. I wanted to make certain that my daughter never suffered because of my lack of knowledge."

"Well, Cassie, your knowledge doesn't seem any more or less than anyone else's with or without a degree. And

I've learned that money and degrees can't guarantee you'll have any brains."

She had to laugh because she'd always thought the same thing. "You're right, I guess," she admitted with a sigh, running a finger of her free hand up and down the rim of her water glass. "I always thought there were more than enough educated idiots to go around. But I guess because I didn't have the advantage of college I want to make certain my daughter has every advantage."

"That's both understandable and commendable, but I don't think you have to worry about Sofie in that area. Or any other," he admitted. "Tomorrow at school, Sofie's going to invite the two boys who have been teasing her to help her with her science project."

"And to a pizza party on Sunday, right?" She laughed again. "My mother always said 'when it doubt, ply them with food.'"

"And mothers are never wrong, at least when it comes to food. No self-respecting male will ever turn down an offer of homemade food, especially pizza." He winked at her. "I didn't, remember?" he said, reminding her that her daughter had invited him to lunch on Sunday as well. "Hopefully after Sunday, Sofie will no longer be seen as someone to be wary of, or envious of or even intimidated by, but someone to help." He smiled. "Simply another…friend."

Cassie was thoughtful for a moment. "Your way sounds so…logical." She grinned. "My first instinct was to rush out and thrash anyone who'd hurt my child."

Beau chuckled. "As any good parent should feel," he commented. "Cassie, no parent knows the answers to every question."

"Yeah, well, do you suppose someone could tell

mothers that *before* they give birth so they don't always feel so…insecure?"

"I'm sure it probably would help. In the meantime, I'm going to work with the two boys who've been involved in this to see if I can't help them in that area."

Cassie smiled, genuinely touched by his concern not just for her daughter, but for the other kids involved as well. "I think it's wonderful that you take such an interest in these kids' well-being." Realizing she was getting too comfortable with her hand in his, she slowly withdrew it, and ran her damp palm down her thighs. "I can't believe that if this works you will have helped Sofie turn what had been adversaries into friends," Cassie said quietly. "Two friends, actually." Unconsciously, she touched the top of his hand. "You're very good at that," she said, before lifting her gaze to meet his. "Turning adversaries into friends. Aren't you?"

Isn't that exactly what he'd done to her? When she'd arrived, she had no intention of letting her relationship with him become anything more than politely perfunctory, a way to help her daughter, yet keep her own distance from him on every level. And yet, now, just a few hours later, there was something different and a bit exhilarating simmering between them, something she wasn't sure she wanted or even understood.

"Cassie." He took her hand again to get her attention. "You look like you've just signed on for a trip to the gallows. Does this accepting help from a neighbor bother you that much?"

"No," she admitted reluctantly, feeling her natural defenses spring to attention. "I…I guess I just don't understand quite what's expected of me." And she never liked not knowing. It was too easy to disappoint someone, too easy to discover someone expected more than she could or would deliver. "What do you get in return?" she asked. She'd learned a long time ago nothing in life was free, especially when it came to male/female relationships.

"Just your friendship, hopefully," he assured her with a smile. He shrugged. "I'll be spending time with Sofie and the other kids for the next month or so, working on her science project, and while I'm doing that hopefully you and I will learn to be…friends." He shrugged. "It's a small town and you can never have too many friends. That's it. That's the extent of my ulterior motives. Sound good?"

"I've got no complaints so far," she admitted hesitantly, wondering why the man stirred up emotions in her she thought long dead and buried.

"Well, then," he said, getting up and setting his napkin on the table, "what do you say we keep it that way?"

Setting her napkin on the table, she stood up, too, hating to see the wonderful evening come to an end. "Thank you for everything tonight, Beau. For dinner, for introducing me to your family, and especially for helping my daughter."

He stepped around the table, and closer to her. "You're welcome, Cassie. It was my pleasure, truly." He chuckled. "Although I must admit you're the first woman to ever thank me for introducing you to my family. Usually women are running the other way."

"Why?" she asked, and he shrugged.

"Apparently eccentricity is not as popular as once believed," he said and she laughed again.

"Well, see, right there that makes me different from other women since I come from a very long line of eccentrics," she admitted with a smile, lovingly thinking of her mom and her aunt. "And I learned a very long time ago to just accept people as they are and not to try to change them to fit some sort of preconceived mold someone else has." Nervous because he was so close and realizing she was babbling, she glanced out the windows and sighed. "I can't believe it finally stopped snowing," she said with a shake of her head.

"But the streets probably haven't been plowed yet, so you'd better leave your car here and let me drive you home."

"But—"

He pressed a finger to her lips. "No buts, Cassie," he said softly. "It's too late, dark and cold for you to be out driving around in this, especially with a child. I'll run you home and in the morning Shorty can return your car so you can get to work." The desire to nestle her face against the warmth and softness of his skin startled her since it was so foreign.

"Okay," she admitted, realizing she wasn't thrilled with the idea of driving.

"I'll just go get the car. I'll have Shorty get your coats."

"And my daughter," she added with a small breath, vividly aware of his continued closeness.

Beau took another step closer to Cassie, drawn to the vulnerable look in her eyes, the need and desire he saw banked there. "Cassie." He wondered what it would be like to watch that need and desire flare in her eyes, in her body as she responded to him, with him... Without thinking, he slid an arm around her waist. She stepped into him and raised her hands to his chest.

His gaze remained on hers as he lowered his head and gently brushed her lips in a feathery light stroke that had her standing on tiptoe, reaching for him.

Frightened by the intensity of the feelings swirling deep inside of him, feelings he'd thought he'd protected himself from years ago, Beau abruptly stepped back, not wanting to think about what he was feeling.

"Be right back," he said as he turned on his heel and swept out of the room. Cassie stood there, staring after him, the lingering taste of him warming her lips and her vulnerable, aching heart.

Chapter Four

The next morning, Sofie burst into her mother's bedroom, jumping on the bed. "Mommy! Mommy! Are you awake yet?" She planted her hands on Cassie's cheeks and pressed her nose close to her mother's. "Mommy, are you still sleeping?"

"Not anymore I'm not." Awake now, Cassie blinked away the last remnants of sleep and laughed, tumbling her daughter over into the bed with her and nuzzling her cheek. She frowned when she caught a glimpse of the bedside clock, nearly going into a panic.

"Oh, my God, Sofie. We're late. It's almost seven. Why aren't you dressed for school yet?" Cassie bolted upright, taking Sofie with her as she rubbed her eyes to clear her vision.

She'd almost overslept and she never overslept. But then again, she normally didn't spend half the night tossing and turning, thinking about a man. Or dreaming about him, she thought with a scowl. But that's what she'd done most of the night. Thoughts of Beau, and the kiss they'd shared, had never been far from her mind, tangling her thoughts and confusing her emotions.

Determined not to even start down that track this morning, she banished Beau from her mind and glanced at the bedside clock again.

"Sofie, we're late. Really late. We've got to move."

"Mama." Sofie giggled and squirmed out of her mother's arms. "We're not late. Honest." Sofie crossed her heart, then grinned. "There's no school today."

"No school?" Cassie repeated, confused. She blinked again. "But it's not Saturday, is it?" she said, realizing she wasn't entirely sure of the day. She'd been so busy the past month with the move, opening the shop, meeting Beau.... No, scratch that last one, she mentally corrected with a frown. Beau had nothing to do with this mental confusion she was feeling, she assured herself. She'd just been busy, very busy. And she'd been having a hard time remembering which day was which simply because she'd packed so much into every single one.

"No, Mama, it's not Saturday. Yet." Sofie giggled, rolling her eyes. "It's only Thursday, but there's no school 'cuz the furnace broke and they don't got any heat, so school called this morning and said they were closed," Sofie announced, bouncing over to the window. "So Grandma's making her famous blueberry pancakes for us and she said we could make a snow fort in the backyard later, too. Mama, are you gonna have some of Grandma's pancakes?" Sofie asked, turning to her. "And do you want to help us build a snow fort?"

"Yes, honey," she said, smiling at Sofie. "I'll have some

pancakes, but I'm afraid I'm going to have to take a rain check on the snow fort." She picked up Sofie and covered her face with kisses. "I still have to go into the shop today." Sofie squealed at her mother's teasing as the doorbell rang. "Who on earth can that be?" Cassie asked and Sofie grinned.

"It's Dr. Beau, Mama. That's why I came to wake you up. Grandma said she invited Dr. Beau for pancakes and she said to tell you that unless you want to have a pajama party for breakfast, you'd better get dressed."

Cassie almost dropped her daughter. "Dr. Beau's here. *Now?*" she almost croaked.

"Uh-huh," Sofie said with a grin and a nod. "I told you, Grandma invited him to breakfast. Isn't that great?"

"Oh…that's just…terrific," Cassie said dully, setting her daughter down safely on her feet. She hadn't intended to see the man first thing this morning. She'd wanted to gather her defenses before she saw him again.

"So are you gonna have breakfast in your jammies, Mama?" Sofie asked and Cassie almost groaned when she glanced down at her wrinkled sleep shirt.

"Uh, no, sweetheart, I don't think so." She took Sofie's hand. "But I'll tell you what, why don't you go down and entertain Dr. Beau until I get dressed? I'll be down in about five minutes." Or less. However long it took her to take a quick shower, throw on some clothes and pull the tangles out of her hair and the sleep out of her eyes.

"'Kay, Mama, we'll save some pancakes for you."

"Do that, sweetheart," Cassie said, opening the bedroom door to let her daughter out, then immediately closing it before dashing into her bathroom to try to make herself presentable.

* * *

"I'll get the door, Grandma," Sofie yelled as she raced down the hall toward the front door.

"Make sure you look to see who it is first, sweetheart," her grandmother cautioned, quietly humming as she flipped another batch of blueberry pancakes, totally content in her kitchen.

"I will, Grandma," Sofie said, peeking out the side window and nearly bouncing out of her tennis shoes. "It's Dr. Beau," Sofie shouted, thrilled. "And Uncle Jasper, and even Shorty." She tugged open the door and grinned at them, nearly breathless with excitement. "Hi, Dr. Beau. Hi, Uncle Jasper. Hi, Shorty." She giggled. "You're full of snow."

Beau grinned back at her, tugging off his gloves and slapping the snow from them. "That's because we've been shoveling," he said, giving her hair a ruffle before loosening his coat and scarf.

"Aye, there you are, little lassie. So how's my favorite little princess this beautiful snowy morning?" Jasper gave Sofie a wink, going down so that he was eye level with her. His gaze shifted then lifted and froze when he spotted Sofie's grandmother coming up the hall.

He could only stare mutely at the vision heading his way in a beautiful flowing green silk caftan, a triple stand of white pearls as snowy white as her hair and a beautiful, angelic face that had to have been carved by the Almighty himself. Jasper swallowed hard, wondering why his throat had gone dust-dry.

"Good morning, dears," the woman caroled gaily, encompassing them with a welcoming smile. "I'm so delighted you could join us for breakfast this morning."

"Well, Miss Gracie, I had to bring Cassie her car anyway, so we appreciate the invitation," Beau said. "It's not every day we get homemade blueberry pancakes, isn't that right, Uncle Jasper?"

Jasper stood there like a statue, his mouth open, his gaze fixed on her. An angel, he thought dimly. His very own angel. In the flesh. After all these years. He simply couldn't believe it. He'd long ago given up hope of ever finding her. But now…now she stood before him and he didn't quite know what to do with himself. His heart did a quick tumble, then began to beat rapidly in his chest, nearly making him breathless.

"Miss Gracie, I'd like you to meet my uncle Jasper. And Shorty."

"Pleased to meet ya, ma'am," Shorty said, snatching off his wool cap and reaching around Jasper to grab her hand firmly, giving it several fast, fierce, welcoming pumps.

Jasper continued to stare, his mouth moving but nothing came out.

Laughing gaily, Gracie lifted a hand to pat his cheek. "Jasper, dear, do close your mouth before you begin collecting flies," she said with a twinkle in her eye. "And before you ask," she went on, "your glasses are right…here." Much like Cassie had done the night before, she reached up and removed his fogged glasses from under his wool hat, tucked the damp hat into the pocket of his coat, then smoothed down the stray strands of white hair standing out on end around his ears, before settling his glasses comfortably on his nose again. "There. That's better," she said, giving him another pat on his cheek. "And Jasper, dear, I made coffee since I know how much you dislike tea." She reached out and rebuttoned his vest, which was buttoned crookedly. Suddenly Gracie slowly lifted her startled gaze to his. They merely stared at each other for a moment and time seemed to still, then stall. Messages were sent, and received, shaking them both.

Gracie patted the strand of pearls around her neck, looking confused.

"Why don't you get these wet, heavy coats off, and then we'll go into the kitchen and have some fresh, hot coffee and a chat. Breakfast is almost ready." Food. That's what was needed right now.

"Is Cassie around?" Beau asked, glancing around.

"Mama's getting dressed," Sofie said with a grin. "'Cuz she didn't want to have a pajama party for breakfast."

"She didn't, did she?" Beau asked with a grin, scooping Sofie up in his arms. "Well, why not I wonder?" he asked, nuzzling his nose against Sofie's and making her giggle and throw her arms around his neck.

"Uhm…yes, she'll be along in a few minutes," Gracie said as she hung their coats in the closet.

Still feeling thunderstruck, Jasper allowed her to lead him into the kitchen, wondering if this joyous feeling, this lightness of the heart, was what it felt like to finally, truly, be in love….

"We got lots and lots of snow out in the yard," Sofie informed them all with a grin as she forked up another bite of pancake from her sticky plate. "And Dr. Beau, did you know we got a tree house in the back?" she asked around a mouthful of food.

"You do?" he asked in surprise, pushing his empty plate away and sipping his steaming coffee before leaning back in his chair, full and content.

"Uh-huh," Sofie said with a nod and a mouthful of food. "My cousin, Rusty, built it with his dad." Something resembling a shadow passed over her, and she glanced down at her plate before glancing up at him again. "Rusty's got a dad now. He didn't have one before. I don't got one, still," she said solemnly. "Rusty used to live here with my grandma and his grandma and his mom before she got married to his dad."

"Katie and Lucas?" Beau asked, glancing at Gracie, hoping to keep all the familial connections straight.

"That's right," Gracie said with a smile. "Louella was so delighted when Katie finally found love again. You know, Beau, it's not easy being a single mother," she said carefully.

"Oh, I know, Miss Gracie, I know," he admitted with a smile. "In my practice I see a lot of single mothers. Single *working* mothers. And believe me, for what they go through they never get enough credit as far as I'm concerned."

"Who's giving me credit and for what?" Cassie asked as she came into the kitchen. She glanced at Beau as she nervously pushed up the sleeves of her uniform, then rounded the table to kiss Jasper and Shorty on the cheeks.

The table might be full of people, but she was only aware, vividly aware, of Beau. She thought of the kiss they'd shared last night and nearly flushed before banishing the thought.

"Good morning," she said with a forced grin as she pulled out her chair, trying not to feel self-conscious at the way Beau's eyes were tracking her. She felt the heat of his gaze warm her right through her sweatshirt.

"Your mom was just telling me how difficult it is to be a single mother," Beau offered, and Cassie almost groaned.

"Mama," she said nervously, wondering what on earth her mother was up to now. No good, probably, she thought with a sigh. "Being a single mother isn't all that much different from being a married mother," Cassie protested with a shrug, reaching for the plate of pancakes and forking several onto her plate.

"Oh, I disagree, Cassie," Beau said, leaning forward in his chair, his gaze intent on her. "Married mothers aren't on duty twenty-four seven. Nor do they have to worry about being the only responsible adult in the household. Or supporting themselves and their kids on their own, alone. Or handling every single situation, problem or emergency that crops up by themselves without any help or support. Not to mention never having a shoulder to cry on or lean on." He hesitated for a moment, his eyes twinkling in a way that made her heart flip. "In my book, single moms are the true heroes of the world. Especially their kids' worlds."

"I was a single mother," Jasper announced, startling the room into an abrupt silence. Realizing everyone had turned to stare at him, Jasper all but flushed. "Well, I was," he blustered nervously, giving his hair an annoyed tug. "Aye, I was all alone when Beau came to me. Did everything on my own, too," he insisted, making Beau and Cassie exchange smiles.

"And what was I, chopped chowder?" Shorty demanded, making Sofie giggle.

"That's funny, Shorty," she said and he turned to her with a wink and a grin. "What's chopped chowder?"

"Don't talk with your mouth full, sweetheart," Cassie cautioned, all but devouring her own pancakes.

Shorty grinned. "Aye, lassie, chopped chowder is just an expression."

"So you said it instead of bad words?" Sofie asked knowingly and Cassie all but gaped at her.

"What do you know about bad words, young lady?" Cassie asked in surprise.

"Uh…nothing, Mama," Sofie said, suddenly interested in her near-empty plate. From under her lashes, she glanced at Beau, who grinned at her. She grinned back.

"I brought your car back, Cassie," Beau said, trying to divert her attention from Sofie and her knowledge of bad words. "But none of the streets have been plowed yet, or if they have been, they've been snowed over again. I had Shorty to pull me out if I got stuck on the drive over here, but you'd be better off if you didn't drive anywhere today."

"I guess I'll just have to hoof it into the salon today," she said with a grin.

"Walk?" Her mother, Jasper and Beau caroled in unison, one more horrified than the other.

Cassie glanced around the table. "Well, you don't have to act like I just announced I was going to dance naked through town," she protested.

Sofie's eyes widened and rounded. "Mama, are you really going to *dance naked?*" Giggling, Sofie covered her mouth with her hand. "Can I watch?"

"Hey, me, too," Beau said, wiggling his brows at Cassie, who flushed.

"It's just an expression, honey," Cassie assured her daughter. "Like…chopped chowder," she added absently, giving Beau a look.

"But you can't possibly be serious, Cassie dear," her mother protested worriedly. "It's frigid out, and the wind is blowing so hard you can barely see in front of you. I know it's only four blocks, but really dear, I don't think you should be out in this weather."

"Wait. Wait. Wait," Beau said, holding up his hand before everyone got into a tizzy. He looked at Cassie and smiled that smile that made her pulse do a wicked two-step. "Cassie, I've got my four-wheel-drive Jeep outside. I'm going into the office anyway, so I can just drop you off at the salon. And when you're ready to come home, I'll just swing by and pick you up. Sound fair?"

"Are you sure it's not too much trouble?" she asked worriedly, realizing once again the man was coming to her rescue. She'd never depended on anyone before, so this was new and foreign territory for her. And she wasn't certain she was entirely comfortable with the idea.

"Cassie," he said, giving her the exasperated look he'd given her last night when he'd given her the "good neighbor" speech. "My office is across the street and three doors down from your shop," he pointed out, as if this was news to her. "And I hardly think it's going to be a hardship to drop you off at the shop since I pass right in front of it on my way into the office anyway. No, it's not too much trouble, or any trouble," he said, stopping any protests she might have made. One brow lifted. "And it *is* the neighborly thing to do," he said, reminding her of her promise last night to try to accept his help simply for what it was: one neighbor helping another. "Life in a small town, remember?"

"I remember," Cassie said dully, realizing her attempts to keep Beau at a distance were failing. Miserably. He said all he wanted was her friendship, but how on earth was she supposed to keep her feelings...friendly when he kept doing things that touched her heart? And kissed her as he had last night?

"Not that I'd mind watching you dance naked down Main Street," he said with a grin. "But I think this way might be a bit warmer."

"Okay," she finally said, realizing this would be easier. She'd rather have a nice, warm ride, than hoof it in this weather.

"Good," Beau said, giving Gracie a comforting wink.

Cassie drained her coffee cup. "If you're finished, though, I'd like to get going," she said, glancing at her watch.

He drained his coffee cup as well. "I'm finished," he said, getting up from the table. "Thank you for breakfast, Miss Gracie," he said going around the table to kiss her cheek, then on impulse kissing Sofie's cheek as well, making her giggle. "Gotta run." He hurried after Cassie, who was already at the closet, retrieving their coats.

The moment Cassie and Beau stepped out the front door, the biting wind slapped at them, nearly toppling Cassie over.

"Good Lord," she muttered, bracing herself and ducking her mouth deeper beneath the scarf she'd wrapped around her neck.

"Be careful," Beau said, taking her arm and holding onto her. "I'm sorry we didn't have time to shovel your walk or the drive before breakfast, but I'm sure Shorty will have it done by the time we get back."

Cassie laughed. "Are you trying to spoil me?" she asked, giving him a sideward glance. "I'm not used to having men come to my rescue, shovel my walk, or drive me around in a blizzard." She shivered, shoving her hands deeper in her coat pockets.

"I don't think there's anything wrong with spoiling a

woman," Beau said quietly, guiding her carefully toward the car and watching how and where he stepped. The snow had packed down and was now coated with an icy film.

"You don't, huh?" she teased. "That may explain why you've got every single woman in Cooper's Cove beating a path to your door."

He groaned as he reached for the car door. "Don't remind me," he said, opening the door for her and helping her in. "I just remembered about Mrs. Vander-whatever," he said with a scowl, making her laugh again.

He came around the car and got in, starting the engine and letting it warm for a few moments so the defrosters could do their work.

Cassie snuggled deeper into her seat and turned to look at him. She'd never considered a car romantic, but he was sitting so close to her, and with the snow and wind blowing around them it was like they were cocooned in their own private world.

"So what are you going to do about her?" Cassie asked. "She's bound to find you, you know, especially once she discovers there's no mumps!"

"Dodge and weave," he admitted with a smile, turning to her. His gaze shifted to her mouth, reminding her of the taste of his lips, and the kiss they'd shared last night. She felt a sudden tug of yearning so deep she sighed, deliberately trying to shake it off.

"Well, from what Shorty said, I think you've had more than enough practice."

"Oh, that I have. I've been dodging and weaving women's clutches since college." He grinned, shifting the car into gear and slowing pulling away from the curb. "Haven't been caught yet."

"So you never considered getting married?" Cassie asked, not certain why she wanted to know. For some reason the thought of Beau being all alone for the rest of his life made her sad.

"Considered it, yes," he admitted quietly. "For one crazy moment back when I was a young, naive intern."

"But you didn't go through with it?"

He shook his head as he flipped on his directional and slowly turned onto a nearly deserted Main Street. "Nope, afraid not. Guess like Uncle Jasper I'm just not the marrying kind."

"I find that hard to believe, considering how good you are with children." She hesitated, knowing she was about to pry and not caring. "What happened? Cold feet?" she asked.

"Not exactly," he said hesitantly. "More of a case of a…cold heart I'd say," he said.

"I don't understand," Cassie said with a shake of her head, truly confused.

"Neither did I, Cassie. Neither did I." Sighing, Beau gripped the wheel tighter as the snow became deeper. "What about you?" he asked, glancing at her. "Ever taken the plunge?"

"No," she said quietly, folding her gloved hands together in her lap. She'd never been ashamed of the fact that she'd fallen in love and conceived a child outside of marriage. The only shame she had was that her judgment had been so poor. But at seventeen, she'd been blinded by love, able to see only what Sofie's father wanted her to see. He'd been sweet and charming, and totally swept her off her feet with declarations of love and happily ever after.

It wasn't until *after* she became pregnant that she

realized behind that charm hid the morals of a snake. She was just grateful Sofie would never have to know what a coward her father had been.

"I've never been married, and quite frankly, never even considered it, at least not since Sofie's birth." She shrugged. "It's not something that's necessary in my life. I have everything I could ever want or need," she said. But the moment the words were out, for an instant, just an instant a flash of hunger and loss for all the things she'd always wanted—a home, a loving husband, more children—and knew she could never have flashed as bright as a flare inside of her.

She couldn't think about that, or about all the things she knew she could never have. To have those fanciful dreams that had fueled her young life would require her to trust a man completely, something she wasn't entirely certain she could ever do again.

And now it wasn't just her heart and life at risk, but Sofie's as well. Putting her heart in jeopardy was one thing, but to even consider putting little Sofie's heart in danger by trusting the wrong man was not a risk Cassie was willing to take.

She'd done everything she could to protect her daughter, and she'd continue to do so as long as there was a breath left in her body.

"Getting married when you already have a child can be a risky proposition for any mother." Beau glanced at her again. "There's a lot more to consider than just yourself and your own well-being. You also have to take into consideration your child's life and well-being, and that can be a pretty scary proposition for any mom. So I can understand your feelings completely," Beau admitted, unknowingly echoing her own thoughts. He pulled to a stop at the curb in front of her salon and merely studied her for a moment, then smiled as he leaned over and tucked a stray strand of hair behind her ear. "You're getting better," he said with a smile and she blinked at him.

"Better?"

"At least you didn't jump when I just touched you. I'd say we're making progress."

"Progress," Cassie repeated with a frown, not certain she liked that word or the unsaid implications.

"Progress as *friends,*" he emphasized at the look on her face. "It shows that maybe, just maybe you're beginning to trust me just a little bit."

"I…guess I am," she reluctantly admitted, then quickly added. "As a friend."

"I take it you haven't had many…male friends?"

She had to think about it for a moment. "Actually, I haven't," she admitted, "but until you mentioned it, I'd never really thought about it before." She sighed. "So much of my life has been devoted to caring for Sofie, I never really had the time or the inclination to have casual friendships, male or female."

"So that explains why you're so skittish," he said with a nod. "But remember what I said last night, Cassie. This is a small town with small-town manners. It's really like one big family, everyone is friends and everyone helps out everyone else. It doesn't mean anyone has ulterior motives."

"Oh, Beau, I know that," she said, immediately feeling guilty. "It's just like I said, I've never had a male friend before so you're going to have to just be patient while I learn the rules and the ropes."

"Patience is one thing I have an abundance of," he assured her with a smile.

"Good." She hesitated for a moment. "Beau." She reached out and laid her hand on his arm. "I can't think of anyone I've ever met that I'd rather have as a friend than you," she said quietly, watching as a myriad of emotions crossed his gorgeous features.

He lifted his hand to her cheek. "And I can't think of anyone else I've ever met that I'd rather have as a friend than you." His thumb began to stroke her tender skin. Closing her eyes, Cassie sighed, then simply relaxed and enjoyed his touch.

Oh, the things this man could do to her heart, she thought dully, letting her eyes flutter open as fear suddenly engulfed her. He was just a friend, she told herself. Nothing more. Nothing less. And neither of them was interested or wanted anything more so there was no reason to be afraid, she assured herself.

"Well, Cass, I'd better get going. I have a feeling I have messages piled sky-high by now. Why don't you just give me a call when you're ready to go home?"

"I will," she promised. He started to open his own door to help her out as she opened the door but she held up her hand to stop him.

"Beau, stay in the car. No sense getting pelted with wind and snow again. " She grinned at him, her eyes twinkling in amusement. "I think I can make it from here to the front door by myself. Really," she insisted when he looked doubtful. "Thanks for everything. I'll see you later." She shut the door before he had a chance to protest.

Why, she wondered, had the man gotten under her skin so quickly? Cassie shook her head as she started up the walk toward the front door of her shop. She didn't know. She only knew that she was going to have to watch her step. Figuratively and literally, she thought with a gasp as her foot almost slid out from under her. The last thing she needed was another bad tumble because of a man. Friend or not.

Chapter Five

Cassie was busy most of the morning, but by two she finally had a break. She was in the back room emptying and reorganizing her storage cabinets when she heard the tinkle of the bell over the front door.

"I'm in back," she called. "I'll be right out."

Wiping off her hands, Cassie hurried to the front of the shop, grinning in delight when she saw her twelve-year-old nephew, Rusty.

"Hi, sweetheart."

"Hi, Aunt Cassie," he said with a grin. "You remember my friend, Sean Hennighan, don't you?" he said, absently waving a hand toward the kid slouching next to him.

Cassie looked at the tall, lanky kid standing next to Rusty and banked a shudder. Boy, she thought with an inner smile, if ever there was a kid that would give a mother heart failure just by a look, it was Sean. The look in the kid's eyes simply screamed mischief and mayhem and not necessarily in that order. Sean came by his reputation honestly and every time Cassie saw the kid she was grateful *she* wasn't his mother.

"Hi, Sean."

"Hi," he mumbled, lifting a hand absently in the air.

"So what brings you here, Rusty?" she asked and he shifted his weight uncomfortably.

"Me and Sean, well…we've sort of gone into business."

"Business?" she repeated skeptically, wondering if it was monkey business as her glance went from one far-too-innocent face to the other. "And, um, does your mom know about this business?" Cassie asked with a lift of her brow.

"Yeah, Aunt Cassie, she does," he said sheepishly. "It's okay with her. Honest," he added earnestly, making her smile.

"I believe you, honey," she fibbed, making a mental note to give Katie a call just to be on the safe side. Not that she didn't believe her nephew, but she'd learned from experience that kids had a way of telling you only *part* of the story *most* of the time.

"So tell me about your business, boys."

"Well, it's kind of a delivery business, and a snow shoveling business," Rusty said, glancing at Sean for approval. He nodded.

As did Cassie. "Okay, I get it. So you're trying to drum up some business and you've come to see if you can shovel my walk?"

"Uh no. Actually Aunt Cassie…" Rusty's voice trailed off and he looked at Sean, who grinned, making a nervous shiver skate over Cassie. That grin had to mean trouble, she was certain of it.

"We've already been hired to shovel your walk." Sean

dug into the pocket of his winter coat and extracted a slightly crushed and wilted rose. He frowned down at it, then tried to press the damaged petals back into place with dirty fingers before handing it to her. "And to deliver this."

Cassie could only stare at the once beautiful, delicate yellow rose in confusion before lifting her gaze to Rusty's. "Honey, I don't understand."

Rusty grinned, shuffling his feet again. "Dr. Beau hired us to deliver that flower to you, and to shovel your walk in front of the shop."

"In back, too," Sean added. "I'm doing the back. Rusty's doing the front."

"Wait a minute," Cassie said, holding up her hand in total confusion. "Are you saying Dr. Beau hired you to shovel *my* sidewalks?"

"And to deliver that thing," Sean added, nodding toward the damaged flower, wanting to make certain she knew they'd done their jobs. All of them.

"But why?" Cassie asked glancing from one to the other in confusion.

The boy's exchanged their own confused glances and shrugs, then Rusty turned to her.

"Beats me, Aunt Cassie," he said, reaching into his own coat pocket. "But Dr. Beau said if you got that funny look on your face, the one like you got right now, I should give you these." Rusty pulled a wrapped lollipop and a crumbled note from his own pocket and handed them to her.

The lollipop made her smile, and as she started to unfold the note, Rusty asked, "Can we go get started now, Aunt Cassie?"

"Sure honey," she said absently. "Go ahead, but make

sure you come in if you get too cold or wet, you hear me? I don't want you getting sick."

"Yeah, we will," Rusty assured her with a grin and a wave of his hand. "We'll stop back in when we're done, too," he added. "Just to make sure you're happy with what we've done."

"Okay, honey, do that."

Still clinging to the delicate if somewhat damaged rose, Cassie read her note, laughing out loud as she read it.

Cassie, don't frown. This isn't a trick or a bribe, merely a thank-you for breakfast from one neighbor to another. Besides, I believe in supporting our youthful entrepreneurs, which hopefully will keep them busy and out of trouble. At least for today. Call me when you're ready to go home.
Beau
P.S. Even a rose that's been bruised and crushed can still be beautiful.

"Oh." Cassie blinked back tears, immeasurably moved by what Beau seemed to be telling her. She couldn't remember the last time a man had given her a flower. Couldn't remember when, if ever, a man seemed to be able to see through her to the deepest secrets and fears she held close to her heart.

"Friends, huh," she murmured with a watery laugh, pressing the soft petals to her lips for a moment and letting her eyes slide closed.

How on earth was she supposed to keep thinking of Beau as just a *friend* when he did so many things that warmed and touched her scarred, wary heart?

* * *

By Sunday morning, Sofie was so excited about her friends coming over and her pizza party, she was driving Cassie, who was elbow deep in pizza dough, crazy.

When the doorbell rang around eleven, Cassie was just putting the last two pizzas in the oven. "Mama, can you get that?" she called and heard Gracie's gentle laugh filter back at her.

Beau, Jasper and Shorty had arrived. Beau and Jasper to help Sofie and the boys with their science project, and Shorty merely to keep an eye on everything else.

"So how's the pizza baking coming?" Beau asked, walking into the kitchen. Cassie turned to him with a smile, realizing her heart did a sudden tumble just at the sight of him. They'd spent a lot of time together the past few days and she had to admit both she and Sofie were enjoying themselves. Beau was a very kind and unusual man.

"Great. I've made six pizzas," she said with a slight frown. "But I'm not sure that's going to be enough."

Beau laughed, leaning against the counter and pinching off a corner of one of the cooling pizzas before popping it in his mouth. He almost swooned. "You're right, Cassie," he said, going for another little piece. "I don't think there'll be enough," he said with a smile as that panicked look came into her eyes. "Easy, easy," he said, reaching out to give her shoulders a comforting squeeze, scrambling her senses and her pulse. "I'm just kidding. There'll be plenty, and if not, we can always call someplace and order more."

"*Order pizza?*" she said with a shudder as if he'd just announced he was going to order fried ferrets. "I'd rather eat cardboard. And besides, Sofie's never had anything but homemade pizza."

He all but gaped at her. "You mean you've always made pizza like this…." He waved his hand around the now messy kitchen. "From scratch?"

"Actually, I always make everything from scratch," she confirmed with a smile, enjoying the stunned look on his face. "Nothing in boxes, bags or cans. No microwave potatoes or popcorn or anything else. Everything I cook is always made from scratch with fresh ingredients. I've always managed to have a garden, even if it was just a small indoor garden, so I could plant and grow my own herbs. I dry the herbs so I'll have them fresh all year long, ditto on tomatoes and fruit. Those I can, along with fresh pesto and fresh tomato sauce."

"So you can cook," he said, his eyes twinkling in surprised amusement. "I mean *really* cook, like a real old-fashioned fifties mom." There was a hint of admiration in his voice, so she could hardly take offense.

"Hey, don't get insulting, and watch that old stuff," she teased, and he grinned, grabbing her by her shoulders again and dragging her close.

"Insulting? Me? A woman who can really and truly cook something that doesn't come in a box, a bag or a can is a goddess in my book." His fingers began to gently caress her tense shoulders, reminding her of what his touch could do to her. "But don't tell Shorty, he might propose."

Laughing, she looked up at him, saw that gorgeous face soften with humor and amusement and felt herself drowning in the depths of those intense blue eyes.

"I think Shorty and I already had that conversation, didn't we?" she teased again, willing her pulse to slow down.

"Yeah, but that was before he knew you were a woman who could really cook. That changes everything."

"It does, huh?" She laughed, placing her hands on his chest for balance, enjoying his pleasant male scent and the warmth of his closeness. "Well, if you like my pizza, wait until you taste my homemade spinach lasagna," she said with a chuckle.

She could feel the heat of him down the length of her whole body and had to control herself not to step closer, not to press herself against all that masculine strength.

Beau tried to ignore the hot rush of desire racing through his veins. It happened every time he got near Cassie. He shouldn't be feeling this tug of desire or the curious flare of something he could swear was yearning. It was ridiculous, really.

She had flour on her chin and nose, red sauce on the full apron tied around her waist, and bits of green herbs clinging to her hair and her fingers, but none of that seemed to matter. Something about her intrinsic feminine scent still clung to her, drawing him like a butterfly to a flame.

He had no idea what it was about Cassie that was so appealing, but lately he'd found himself unable to fall asleep at night because he'd be thinking about her, reliving their too-brief kiss. Just the thought of it sent his pulse hammering and the blood rushing hotly through his veins.

But it was more than just the physical yearnings that were getting to him. It was the way thoughts of her and Sofie hovered in his mind, catching him off guard at odd moments.

He couldn't even begin to count the number of times he'd caught himself daydreaming about them—both of them—during the day while examining patients, or found himself smiling over the memory of something Cassie or Sofie had said or done.

For the first time since his disastrous relationship in

college he could imagine having a family of his own, and he found himself actually thinking about what it would be like to come home to Sofie and Cassie every night.

Those thoughts terrified him because he felt in his heart that no matter how much he might want to, he couldn't truly ever trust a woman enough to simply believe she loved him for him and not for some ulterior motive. And he didn't know if Cassie could ever trust anyone—any man—totally. But he *did* know that you couldn't have any kind of relationship without trust as a foundation.

He had to admit he'd never actually met a woman like Cassie. Fiercely independent almost to a fault, she was also honest, blunt and not about to put up with any nonsense from anyone.

Clearly, she was a woman who was determined to succeed at everything she did—without anyone's help.

She was quite a refreshing change from the women he'd been dodging most of his life. She had also made it clear, very clear, that she wasn't interested in any kind of relationship with him, at least nothing more than a friendship. And she couldn't care less how much money he had.

While other women looked at him and saw dollar signs, he wasn't even sure Cassie had any idea how much he was *really* worth. And he had a feeling that if she did know, it might scare her into bolting as fast and as far away as she could get. Sometimes, the mere thought of how wealthy he truly was scared *him,* simply because it was such an awesome responsibility.

"Mama." Sofie dashed into the kitchen then skidded to a halt before crashing into them. "My friends are here. My friends are here. Could you come meet them?" Sofie's glance shifted to Beau's. "And you too, Dr. Beau," she said, her dark brows drawing together suddenly. "Are you gonna kiss my mom?" she asked abruptly, looking up at them with wide, curious eyes.

Cassie froze and tried to step back, but Beau held onto her shoulders. "Would that upset you, Sofie? If I kissed your mother?"

Sofie thought about it for a moment, then shook her head, sending her dark hair flying around her face. "Nah. Dr. Beau, you can kiss Mama, I don't care." Sofie planted her small hands on her hips. "But could you please hurry up 'cuz my friends are waiting?" Before either could say another word, Sofie dashed back out of the kitchen.

"Well, you heard the little lady," Beau said softly, his gaze holding Cassie's while he slowly lowered his mouth to hers. "It's okay with her as long as I…hurry up."

But there was no hurry, nor any hesitancy, as Beau covered Cassie's mouth with his own. Cassie slid her hands up his chest to link behind his neck, pressing herself against him. Beau tightened his arms around her slender waist as surprise, pleasure, then pure male need rocked through his system, nearly knocking the staid, stable doctor off balance.

He'd never before felt this feeling, he was almost certain of it. He'd kissed lots of women over the years and had never given it another thought.

But this was something foreign, this feeling that somehow, some way this was what he was supposed to feel, the way it was supposed to be. The way a man was supposed to feel about his mate.

The thought caused alarm bells to clang loudly in his head, but he ignored them, the pull of Cassie and this incredible feeling were far stronger than the warnings he knew he should heed.

Cassie moaned and shifted her weight, trying to get closer to Beau as his tongue gently teased, caressed and all but seduced hers. Moaning softly, she inched higher on tiptoe, tightened her arms around him and just let herself go—enjoying for a moment, just a moment, something she knew she had no business enjoying.

But it had been so long since she'd felt this purely feminine need tugging at her, so long since she'd felt safe in a man's arms. And that, she realized a bit belatedly, was part of Beau's allure. For some reason, and she simply couldn't think clearly right now to fathom why, Beau made her feel safe.

No man ever had. Not ever. And she feared it was a feeling she couldn't trust.

Reluctantly, she started to draw back, to step back and unwind her arms from around his neck. Obviously as reluctant as she for the kiss to end, Beau followed her lips with his, brushing soft kisses across her mouth as she tried to disentangle herself.

"Beau," she murmured, shaking her head to clear it. Her pulse was hammering like crazy and her entire body was suffused with warmth. "Beau."

"Sorry, Cassie," he said with a tender smile. "I didn't mean to scare you."

"You didn't," she said quickly, licking her lips and still feeling the warmth of him, still able to taste him. "You didn't scare me," she clarified, twisting her nervous hands together. "I guess the feelings you aroused did," she admitted self-consciously, glancing up at him.

"Well, if it's any consolation, I'm having the same problem," he admitted with a wry grin, running his shaky fingers through his dark hair. And it was true. His feelings terrified him simply because he thought he'd grown immune to women and had trained himself not to feel anything.

In truth, what had happened to him in college had not just devastated him, it had also embarrassed him because he'd been so darn foolish and naive, falling for a pretty face and little more. Yes, he'd been young, but that didn't account for his stupidity. He should have known better, but it had never occurred to him at that time that someone would want him simply for his fortune. Now, he was older and wiser and understood that money was a powerful motivator for a lot of women.

"Mama!" Sofie skidded to a halt in the doorway again, hair flying. "Are you coming? Come on, come on, everybody's waiting."

"I'm coming, sweetheart," Cassie said with a smile, turning to her daughter. "I'll be right there."

"Dr. Beau, too?"

"Dr. Beau, too," he answered for himself, casually draping a friendly arm around Cassie's shoulders, not wanting to let her go quite yet. He gave her shoulders a gentle squeeze and smiled at her. "Let's go greet the troops."

"The solar system, Mama, isn't that great?" Sofie asked sleepily as Cassie tucked her in that night. "Me and Brian and Timmy are gonna make a small copy—"

"You mean a replica?" Cassie asked with a smile, brushing Sofie's dark hair off her face. "A replica means a copy of something."

"Yeah, a…replica." Sofie said the word slowly, trying it out on her tongue. "We're gonna make a replica of the solar system for the science fair and Dr. Beau and Jasper are gonna help us."

"That's wonderful, honey," Cassie said, tucking the covers under Sofie's chin. It was almost an hour past her bedtime, but Sofie had been so wound up after her friends left that it had been almost impossible to calm her down. Cassie had let her stay up a bit longer tonight so that she'd have a chance to simply wind down before climbing into bed.

Her mother and Jasper had gone out for ice cream, and Beau was waiting in the living room.

"You could help, too, Mama," Sofie said around a yawn, rubbing a fist against her tired eye.

"Well, thank you, sweetheart," Cassie said, forcing a smile and trying to hide the fact that the idea of helping her daughter prepare a science project, a replica of the entire solar system, terrified her because she knew so little about it. But then again, she thought with an inner smile, that's what libraries were for. She made a mental note to give the librarian a call tomorrow to see what was available on the solar system. And then said a silent prayer of thanks for all of Beau's help.

"Mama?"

"Yes, honey?"

"Do you like Dr. Beau?" Sofie asked, snuggling deeper under the covers.

Just the mention of Beau's name made Cassie smile, she couldn't help it. "Why of course I like Dr. Beau, honey. He's a very nice man."

Sofie nodded as her eyes drooped. "I like him, too, Mama." She frowned a bit, rolling the satin edging on the blanket back and forth in her little fingers. "Mama, do you think we could get married sometime?"

Cassie merely stared at her daughter, surprised by the

question, then she remembered what Beau had said about simply asking her child if something was bothering her. Clearly from the look on Sofie's face this was something that had been on her mind.

"Married, honey?" Cassie repeated in surprise and Sofie bobbed her head.

"Yeah, like Aunt Katie got married to Uncle Lucas."

"Why do you want us to get married?" Cassie asked gently, brushing Sofie's hair off her face.

"So that I could get a daddy, too, like Rusty got. When his mom married Uncle Lucas, he got a daddy."

"And you want me to get married so you can have a daddy, is that what you're saying, honey?" Cassie asked in concern, not quite sure where this was going. Sofie bobbed her head again.

"Well, kinda, I mean I never had a daddy, Mama, and I think maybe I'd like one."

"I see," Cassie said, torn between telling her daughter the truth about her irresponsible father and trying to protect her. But she'd never lied to Sofie, and she wasn't going to start now. She'd simply just have to choose her words carefully.

"Well, sweetheart, you actually do have a daddy." Until this moment, Sofie had never once mentioned wanting a father. Cassie figured when the time came, when Sofie was old enough to understand, she'd explain the entire situation to her.

She hadn't expected that time to come this evening.

"I do?" Eyes wide in excitement, Sofie bolted up in bed, then frowned. "If I got a daddy, how come I don't know him? And how come he doesn't live with us like Uncle Lucas lives with Rusty and Aunt Katie?"

Out of the mouths of babes, Cassie thought with a sigh,

then smiled at her daughter. "Well, honey, I guess that's because there are all kinds of daddies."

"There are?"

Cassie nodded. "Yes, sweetheart. Some daddies live with their kids—"

"Like Uncle Lucas?"

"Yes, honey, like Uncle Lucas. And some daddies don't live with their kids, they live somewhere else—"

"Like my daddy, right?"

"That's right, honey. And some daddies live with just their kids—"

"You mean like without a mama?" Sofie asked with another little frown and Cassie nodded again.

"Yes, honey, without a mama."

"I don't think I'd like that," Sofie announced with a scowl. "I don't want to live with anyone but you and Grandma," Sofie said fiercely, throwing her arms around her mother's neck and holding on. "I love you, Mama, and never want to live with anyone else, not ever."

Cassie hugged her daughter tightly. "That's not something you ever have to worry about, honey. You will always live with me." She'd made certain of it.

When Cassie found out she was pregnant, Sofie's irresponsible father and his family had made her life a nightmare, as if she'd deliberately gotten pregnant. At the time, she'd been too young and inexperienced to realize the smooth charm and loving promises were merely an act, a well-practiced act.

The happily-ever-after she was certain she'd have with Sofie's father had lasted only as long as it took for her to announce her pregnancy. Within hours, his family had come down on her. When they demanded she terminate the pregnancy, offering to make it worth her while, she'd been horrified. They expected her to give up her own child for *their* money?

Were they crazy?

She kept hoping it was all a big mistake, hoping that Sofie's father would step up and do the right thing. When he didn't, when he said he agreed with his family, she knew what a dreadful mistake she'd made.

She was seventeen years old, about to start her senior year of high school and had plans to attend college after graduation. Then everything in her life abruptly detoured simply because she'd been naive enough to fall madly, hopelessly in love with an immature selfish boy who thought having a child was of no more importance than buying a pair of socks.

Even now, after almost seven years, she could still remember the devastation of that moment, could still remember how alone and terrified she'd been. And how humiliated that she'd been so blindly foolish.

It was then that her fierce mother's instinct kicked in. She was not going to terminate her pregnancy, not for him, his family or his money. This was *her* child. And she'd loved her baby from the moment she learned she was expecting. Loved it with a fierce, protective love that only a mother can experience. And so she'd proudly told Sofie's father and his family exactly what they could do with their money.

Cassie had known from that moment forward that everything she did in her life, every decision she made would be made putting her child's interest first. And every action would be solely for the welfare of her child. It would be up to her to provide for her child, to give her baby everything in the world every other child had, and that included an abundance of love.

When she refused the money, Sofie's father's family promised to ruin her and her mother if she ever tried to claim Sofie's true paternity.

As if she'd be announcing to the world that she had allowed herself to be lied to, tricked and basically conned by a selfish, self-centered, immature boy whose only interest was in his own immediate pleasure. And to think she had actually believed he loved her.

Only later did she realize Sofie's father wasn't capable of loving anyone but himself. And that alone was enough of a reason not to want him in her child's life.

Ah, the foolishness of youth, Cassie thought not for the first time. One mistake, one lapse in judgment, had seriously altered not only her life but her precious child's as well.

And she'd been trying to make it up to her daughter ever since, which was probably why she hadn't even contemplated getting involved with another man.

Quite frankly, the thought terrified her. Sofie was old enough now to understand about relationships, and Cassie simply wouldn't risk having her daughter get attached to someone who didn't have her absolute best interests at heart. Or who was merely toying with their feelings and would walk away without a thought.

Cassie would never put her daughter's fragile heart at risk, or do anything to jeopardize Sofie's happiness, not after all these years of struggling to ensure it. To do anything less would be irresponsible, and one thing Cassie prided herself on was her *responsibility*.

Cassie sighed. But in order to ensure her daughter's safety and security, she had signed away Sofie's birth rights, denying her real paternity for posterity.

Not that it mattered, then or now. Cassie wasn't in the

least bit interested in Sofie's father's money, power, or position. All she wanted was to ensure her daughter's future would not involve her father.

At the time it had seemed like the right thing to do, the *only* thing to do.

And Cassie had never regretted signing the papers that would banish Sofie's father from her life forever.

Looking at her beautiful daughter's face now, Cassie knew in her heart, she'd made the right decision, the only decision.

Grinning, she kissed her daughter's forehead. "And I don't want you to live with anyone but me. Ever, either." She tickled Sofie's tummy, making her giggle. "Not even when you get married."

"Yuk," Sofie complained. "I'm never getting married 'cuz then I'd have to go live with a boy."

"Oh, but you want me to get married, huh?" Cassie teased with a grin.

"Yeah. Mama?" Sofie drew back to look at her. "Do you think maybe it would be all right if I prayed for another daddy? A new daddy? One who'd live with us like Uncle Lucas?"

Cassie felt her heart begin to ache just a little bit. "Sure, honey," she said. "I think it would be all right." All the prayer and pleas in the world weren't going to make it happen, but there was no sense hurting her daughter's feelings or dashing her hopes.

"So you'll think about us getting married?" Sofie asked hopefully and Cassie merely sighed again.

"Who's getting married?" Beau asked from the doorway, his brow lifted.

"Mama, maybe," Sofie said, turning to him with a grin and missing the questioning lift of his brow.

"Something you want to tell me, Cassie?" Beau asked with a smile as he came into the room. He felt as if the smile had been flash-frozen on his face. He had no idea why the thought of Cassie marrying *someone else* had sent strong anger surging through him. He didn't want Cassie with another man, and he sure didn't want another man playing father to Sofie.

Realizing the train of his thoughts, Beau dragged a hand through his hair, shocked. What on earth was wrong with him? If he didn't know better he'd say he was jealous. And he'd never been jealous in his life. So this, too, was a new feeling, one he wasn't sure he liked. All he knew was that he was getting used to having Sofie and Cassie in his life, getting used to having them around. And quite frankly, the idea of losing them now frightened him so much he simply couldn't think about it.

"Nope, I've got nothing to tell," Cassie said with a laugh, wanting to avoid this particular conversation with Beau, at least for the moment. "Nothing other than it's time for this munchkin to go to sleep." She lifted the covers and tucked them around her daughter. "You've got school in the morning, sweetheart, and if you don't go to sleep you're going to have a hard time getting up in the morning."

"I know," Sofie admitted stifling a yawn. "But Mama, would you think about what I asked?" Sofie lifted her hands to her mother's cheeks. "Please?"

"Yes, honey," Cassie said quietly. "I promise I'll…think about it." She gave her daughter one final kiss on the cheek.

"Good," Sofie said sleepily, turning on her side. "Night, Mama. Night Dr. Beau."

"Night, sweetheart," Cassie said, getting up from the bed.

Play the Lucky Hearts Game

and get...
2 FREE BOOKS
and a **FREE MYSTERY GIFT...**
YOURS to KEEP!

yes! I have scratched off the silver card. Please send me my **2 FREE BOOKS** and **FREE mystery GIFT**. I understand that I am under no obligation to purchase any books as explained on the back of this card.

Scratch Here!
then look below to see what your cards get you... 2 Free Books & a Free Mystery Gift!

310 SDL EEXL   210 SDL EEWA

FIRST NAME   LAST NAME

ADDRESS

APT.#   CITY

STATE/PROV.   ZIP/POSTAL CODE   (S-R-04/06)

Twenty-one gets you **2 FREE BOOKS** and a **FREE MYSTERY GIFT!**

Twenty gets you **2 FREE BOOKS!**

Nineteen gets you **1 FREE BOOK!**

TRY AGAIN!

Offer limited to one per household and not valid to current Silhouette Romance® subscribers. All orders subject to approval. Please allow 4-6 weeks for delivery.

The Silhouette Reader Service™ — Here's how it works:

Accepting your 2 free books and gift places you under no obligation to buy anything. You may keep the books and gift and return the shipping statement marked "cancel." If you do not cancel, about a month later we'll send you 4 additional books and bill you just $3.57 each in the U.S., or $4.05 each in Canada, plus 25¢ shipping & handling per book and applicable taxes if any.* That's the complete price and — compared to cover prices of $4.25 each in the U.S. and $4.99 each in Canada — it's quite a bargain! You may cancel at any time, but if you choose to continue, every month we'll send you 4 more books, which you may either purchase at the discount price or return to us and cancel your subscription.

*Terms and prices subject to change without notice. Sales tax applicable in N.Y. Canadian residents will be charged applicable provincial taxes and GST. Credit or debit balances in a customer's account(s) may be offset by any other outstanding balance owed by or to the customer.

"Night, Sofie," Beau said, waiting for Cassie and slipping an arm casually around her waist. Cassie paused in the doorway, Beau's arm warm and comfortable around her, and watched her daughter for a moment. Looking at Sofie, she was nearly overwhelmed by love.

After all this time, although she'd love to provide Sofie with a father, a *real* father in every sense of the word, Cassie knew that having a real father for her daughter meant she'd have to make that leap and trust a man enough to let herself fall in love with him. And that thought terrified her.

Cassie glanced at Beau and her heart flipped over and seemed to shudder back into place. And she realized that maybe it was already too late. She hadn't done a very good job of keeping her feelings in check when it came to him.

But she knew better. Had to do better.

For her sake and Sofie's.

Chapter Six

As February flowed slowly into March, temperatures warmed a bit, but not enough for the cautious residents of Cooper's Cove to hail the onset of spring just yet.

For Cassie it seemed as if every waking moment was spent either at the shop, or helping out with Sofie's science project.

Ms. Pringle, the town librarian, had sent over several books on the solar system for Cassie to study with a stern admonishment that it was science fair project time in town and science books were at a premium. She sternly admonished that the books were to be returned promptly. Or else.

Cassie feared the woman too much to ask what the "or else" was, so she made sure she walked the books back to the library a day before they were due—just to be on the safe side.

She wasn't quite sure how or when it had happened, but sometime during the past month she and her mom and Sofie had begun having dinner with Beau, Jasper and Shorty several times a week. It just seemed easiest with Beau and Jasper helping Sofie with her project and Jasper and her mom spending almost every other waking moment together.

Apparently there was a great deal more involved with building an exact replica of the solar system than Cassie had ever envisioned, judging by the number of hours everyone was putting into the project.

At times it seemed as if they were all one big, happy family. And that left Cassie feeling a bit confused.

She'd had a hard time keeping her feelings for Beau in check when she wasn't seeing him nearly every day, and now that she was seeing him so often, it was getting harder and harder to control all the emotions Beau evoked.

They were still just friends in spite of all the time they'd spent together, so Cassie decided that she just wasn't going to think about her feelings anymore.

In keeping with her plans to update and renovate the shop, Cassie had arranged to have the wood floors refinished one day in late March. She'd specifically not booked any appointments past two on that day so the workers could have the shop to themselves that afternoon. But on the afternoon they were due to arrive, Cassie was unusually busy and completely forgot they were coming. She had hired two new stylists, as well as a new nail tech, and word of mouth about all the new services she was offering had spread like wildfire. Now her clientele wasn't just residents of Cooper's Cove, but women from the surrounding towns as well. Business was booming and she couldn't be happier.

Not wanting to turn away any business, she still had a shop full of customers when the floor finishing crew arrived shortly after two. She merely stared at the crew manager in shock when he stomped up to her styling station.

"Lady, what are you doing?" He glanced around the crowded shop with a scowl. "You gotta get rid of everyone. We can't work around all these people. Plus the fumes can be toxic. You gotta close the joint down."

Cassie merely stared at him in shock. "You're kidding," she said nervously, glancing up from the comb-out she was doing. Mrs. Parsons, the reverend's wife, was a stickler about her comb-outs, so Cassie was always particularly careful and attentive when the woman was in her chair.

"Do I look like I'm kidding?" he asked with another scowl, glancing around at all the women. "Look, if you don't get rid of all these people, we can't do the floor." He turned and started to head toward the door with his crew on his heels. "You'll have to reschedule."

"No. Wait." Cassie grabbed his arm, catching a corner of his blue uniform shirt. "Are you sure I have to close?" she asked weakly, and he all but glowered at her, heaving a heavy, put-upon sigh.

"Look, lady, do I ask you if you're sure you know how to do your job?"

"Okay. Okay." She bit her lower lip. "Can you give me…fifteen minutes?" She brightened as his scowl deepened. "Tell you what, there's a diner right down the street. Take your crew down there for some coffee. Tell Patience, she's the lady behind the counter, it's on me."

"On you?" One brow rose as he considered. Finally, he shook his head, then lifted his Red Bull cap to scratch absently at his balding red head. "All right, fifteen minutes. But if this joint ain't cleared out by then, we'll have to head to our next job and you'll have to reschedule."

"It will be. Thanks." Cassie offered him a weak smile,

aware that everyone in the shop had heard their exchange, and was now waiting for her to…good Lord…kick them all out.

She quickly finished Mrs. Parsons' comb-out, and was just shooing the last customer out the door when both the floor refinishers and Beau walked in, one right after the other.

"Lady, I warned you," the refinisher said, giving Beau a look. Not wanting to irritate the man further, Cassie grabbed Beau's arm.

"Come on," she said, grabbing her coat and all but dragging Beau out the door. "We have to leave."

"Is the building on fire or what?" he asked with a grin, knowing Cassie never did anything impulsively.

"Uh, no, but the men are here to redo the floor and they won't do it unless the shop's empty."

"Ahh, I got it," he said, taking her hand as they started walking down Main Street toward his office. "So you have to close?" She nodded and he frowned. "What on earth did you do with all your clients? When I passed by on my way to lunch, you looked like you had a mob in there."

"I did," she admitted with a laugh, trying to relax as the touch of his hand flooded her with a now familiar, welcome warmth. "But I haven't scheduled any appointments for the rest of the afternoon so the shop could be closed."

"So what are you doing for the rest of the day?"

"I don't know," Cassie admitted in surprise, then she grinned. "I'm free," she said, realizing she couldn't remember when she'd had a free afternoon. Immediately a million things she had to do filled her mind and she tried to categorize them by order of importance.

"Cassie?" Her mind stopped and she glanced at him. "Yes."

He paused in front of the back door to his office to look

at her. "Today's Wednesday and my office here in town is closed this afternoon, too."

"And?"

"And I was wondering if you'd like to play hooky? Together?" He wiggled his brows at her, making her laugh. "Just me and you?"

"Play hooky?" she repeated, pretending to be shocked by the mischievous twinkle in his eyes. "I don't think I've ever played hooky," she admitted, warming to the idea. "I was always so disgustingly responsible." Except for one time, her mind reminded her. But she didn't think one afternoon of playing hooky would doom her.

"Was?" he repeated with a lift of his brow that had her whacking his arm.

"Okay, okay, maybe I still am," she admitted with a grin. "It's in my genes I guess. I take after Mama that way. She may be a psychic and eccentric, but she's also the most responsible, reliable person I've ever met."

"Next to you," Beau added.

"Right." She shrugged. "I guess I'm doomed to be responsible and boring." She wasn't certain even she liked the way that sounded.

"Nothing wrong with responsible and boring, Cass. Nothing at all." He grinned. "Okay, let me just go in and close up, and then we'll be on our way, okay?"

"Hey, I'm new at this hooky stuff, you're the expert. Just lead and I'll follow."

"Sounds like a plan to me."

"A matinee?" Cassie said skeptically as Beau pulled into the movie theater parking lot a few minutes later. "You're kidding?"

He grinned. "Nope, I'd never kid about movies." He leaned forward and caught her off guard, brushing his lips against hers in a quick kiss that sent her thoughts and her pulse scrambling. "I'm a huge movie fan, Cassie. Huge." He glanced at the dashboard clock. "We've got about half an hour before the movie starts. I thought we'd grab a couple of hot dogs, a tub of popcorn—"

"Extra butter?" she asked hopefully and he nodded.

"Absolutely," he assured her. "Some drinks and maybe even a box or two of candy and make an afternoon of it."

Still a bit befuddled by his quick kiss, Cassie grinned. "Beau, I haven't been to a movie in the middle of the day since I was a kid." She sighed. "Growing up, Katie and I did everything together. We were more like sisters than cousins. Anyway, every Saturday morning we'd do our chores and promptly at eleven we'd both walk to the Astrology Parlor to get our allowances from our mothers. Then we'd hit the diner for lunch before going to the Saturday afternoon matinee. We'd save up enough money during the week from our lunches to get popcorn and chocolate-covered raisins." Cassie laughed at the memory. "It was wonderful."

"Sounds like it," he said, sounding a bit wistful. She turned to look at him curiously.

"Don't tell me you never went to a Saturday matinee when you were younger?"

"Nope. Never."

"But why?" she asked in surprise.

Beau glanced out the window, then back at her. "Remember when I told you I was teased as a kid?" She nodded. "That was a bit of an understatement. Every class has the one kid that's the outcast, the one kid everyone picks on. In my class, I was it. No one wanted to be on the same planet as me, let alone be seen at a movie matinee with me."

"Oh, Beau, I'm sure that's not true," she said, instantly laying a hand on his arm in comfort.

"Oh, but it was true, Cass. All through school I was known as 'Fatty Four-Eyes.' I was the fat kid who wore thick glasses, aced every class and lived with my eccentric uncle in a spooky old mansion on the outskirts of town." He laughed, but the sound held no mirth. "I'd say that was more than enough to make me the school outcast and the butt of everyone's jokes."

Moved, her heart aching, Cassie laid her hand on his cheek. "Beau, I'm sorry, truly sorry. What a horrible, horrible thing that must have been to endure." And a lonely thing, she realized, her heart literally hurting for him. And yet she didn't hear any bitterness in his voice. None. She drew back and looked in his eyes. "Is that why it's so important to you to make sure other kids aren't teased or bullied? Is that why you're so interested in this subject?" Now, it was beginning to make sense.

"Yeah, I imagine it is." He glanced away for a moment. And why he'd been hesitant to have children of his own. It wasn't just the idea that he might screw up as a parent that scared him spitless. It was also the chance that one of his own children might have to endure the agony that had been his childhood.

"I know firsthand how hurtful and lonely it is to be the butt of everyone's jokes, to live with that dread in your gut, knowing that the minute you enter the playground, and for the next eight to ten hours, day after day, you're going to be teased, picked on, humiliated and bullied. At the time, you don't exactly know what it is about you that causes everyone else to make fun of you, to deliberately hurt you both emotionally and physically. But almost everyone is doing the same things, since bullying and teasing is generally a 'group' mentality. All it takes is one, usually the ringleader, to start and then everyone else follows. The sad thing is, ten years later the kids who did the bullying and the teasing will barely remember it. Yet the child who was the butt of such abuse will endure lifelong self-image and self-esteem issues, as well as trust issues. And if he or she doesn't get counseling, they can turn all that anger into something very destructive." Beau shook his head. "The only peace I ever got was during the summers when I didn't have to go to school."

"Couldn't Uncle Jasper have done something?" Cassie asked quietly and Beau shook his head.

"I never really told him, Cass," he admitted quietly. "And I learned when I began studying this problem that most kids never tell their parents they're going through it, either." He shrugged. "It's embarrassing for kids to admit to their own family, especially their parents, that they're not liked or that they have no friends, or that everyone at school thinks they're weird. All parents want and hope their kids will be liked, accepted and popular. Kids know that, and they simply don't want to disappoint their parents. They also think that by telling an adult, or 'tattling,' it will only increase their problem. And it usually does if adults don't handle it correctly. " He sighed. "Uncle Jasper was truly a wonderful parent, especially considering he never had any children of his own. I couldn't tell him what was going on, Cass, because I knew he'd be hurt by what was happening to me, and he'd blame himself. This is not the kind of thing he would ever be able to understand."

"He is such a sweetheart," Cassie said, feeling a rush of affection for Uncle Jasper.

"Then, Cass, there are those parents who are told and who really don't take their child's complaints seriously. They tell their kids to 'toughen up' or 'ignore' the kids, but trust me it's not that easy."

"I can't even imagine a parent doing that," Cassie admitted with a shake of her head, knowing how horrified she had been when Sofie told her she'd been teased. But, before her own experience with her daughter, she'd never really thought about how awful it must be to be the brunt of something so debilitating and destructive.

"Since I've spent so many years studying this problem, I realize the root cause of teasing and bullying. But at the time I didn't know why this was happening to me."

"Oh, Beau." She touched his cheek, wishing she could take away all the lingering pain and appreciating once again how wonderful and generous he'd been in trying to protect her daughter from the same fate. "I really am sorry. I don't think even adults realized the seriousness of this problem until kids starting turning violent as a result of being teased and bullied at school."

"Yeah, I'll admit that was a stunner even for me. But, Cass, when kids are being bullied and teased, you have to understand they frequently feel cornered. They feel like the situation is hopeless and there is no way out of the nightmare. And for some, violence—taking out the people who are deliberately and intentionally making their life a living nightmare—seems like the only viable option. I've been there, so I know how deep the frustration can run, how deep the wish that it will all just go away is, but I can't stress enough that violence is never the answer." He reached out and brushed a strand of hair from her cheek. "When we were growing up it was a different time and place, Cass. Violence wasn't the first answer to every problem, thankfully. And there was a great deal more compassion for others than there is now. But at least in the years since kids have turned to violence, adults and the authorities have finally realized just how serious this problem has become and how damaging it can be to their children. We've made great strides in trying to prevent bullying and its resulting violence from happening in schools, but we've also made strides in trying to understand the underlying causes. Things aren't perfect yet, but at least we're getting somewhere." He grinned suddenly, that heart-stopping grin that made her aching heart do a wicked dance in her chest. "I was fortunate, Cass, very fortunate."

"How?" she asked, not thinking he was at all fortunate, considering.

"For as long as I can remember Uncle Jasper has always told me never, ever to worry about what anyone else thought or said about me. That the only person whose opinion mattered was my own."

"So how did that help?" Cassie asked with a frown.

"It helped because no matter what the kids said or did, even though it might have been uncomfortable and unpleasant at times, it never really did much damage to my self-image simply because I'd been taught at such an early age not to care what others' opinions were."

"Beau, why do you think Uncle Jasper instilled that in you?" she asked, remembering the first night she and Sofie had dined with Beau and Uncle Jasper and Uncle Jasper had told Sofie it didn't matter what others said or thought of her: smart was a good thing. Cassie couldn't help but smile in affection for Uncle Jasper.

Beau thought about it for a moment. "I think because both he and my dad were immigrants and were both considered a bit eccentric, Uncle Jasper knew that I might suffer from the same fate—labeled odd or eccentric. And I think he wanted me to know that it was only my ability to look in the mirror and make sure I could face myself over my behavior and deeds that was important to him. And the taunts didn't last forever, Cass. When I turned nineteen it was like a miracle happened and things turned around almost overnight."

"Yeah, but nineteen years is a very long time to have to endure such pain." And had to have left lingering scars, Cassie thought. "What changed at nineteen?" she asked, not certain she understood.

"Well, for one thing, I joined the track team my freshman year in college, and over that first year, I lost almost fifty pounds."

"Wow."

"Yeah, it happened so gradually, I guess I never really paid that much attention. Since I couldn't run with my glasses on I had to get contacts as well."

"So you lost fifty pounds, and your glasses and what? When you came home for the summer, every woman in town suddenly realized you were a gorgeous god?" she asked with a grin, imagining it.

He chuckled. "Uh, no, Cass, that didn't happen until I turned twenty-one."

She frowned. "Okay, I'll bite, what happened at twenty-one?"

"Neither my looks, my body, nor my interests had changed, but I *did* inherit my late father's entire estate." He hesitated for a moment. "At the time it was about fifty million dollars." His grin widened as her face all but drained of color. *"That's* when every woman decided I was a, as you say, gorgeous god." Shaking his head, he laughed. "A gorgeous, *rich* god," he clarified, only horrifying her more. "And definitely at the top of the list of every available female."

She drew back and stared at him, horrified. "Are you telling me that just because you had money, women thought you were suddenly appealing?"

He chuckled. "Hey, money, like alcohol, tends to make people see things differently."

"That's disgusting," she said, then realized exactly what he'd just told her. She turned to him, hoping she could find her voice. "Beau, did you just say you inherited *fifty million dollars? American* dollars?" she asked, her voice squeaking upward in shock.

"Uh, actually, by the time all was said and done it was probably closer to seventy million, but who's counting?" he teased, enjoying her shock.

"And you were only twenty-one when you inherited all of this?" Cassie repeated, then shook her head. "You were comfortable with that?" The mere idea of all that money terrified her.

"Hell, no," he said with a laugh, shaking his head. "It scared me spitless, Cassie. All that money is an awesome responsibility. Not to mention the advisors, financial planners, stock brokers and all the other nonsense that goes along with managing a great deal of money."

"Unbelievable," Cassie said, realizing just how different they really were. They'd grown up in the same small town and yet it seemed as if they'd lived in two different worlds. "So what did you do?" she asked.

"I told Uncle Jasper the truth," he said simply. "I just wasn't comfortable with all that money, and in typical Uncle Jasper fashion he scowled, tugged on his hair and said, 'Well, laddie, let's just give it all away then and be done with it.'"

Cassie laughed. "I can actually picture him saying that," she said. "So what happened?"

Beau shrugged. "We gave it all away, or rather most of it. Uncle Jasper and I told the trust officers what we wanted to do—"

"Which was?"

"Put the money to good use, share it with others who didn't even have the basic necessities in life. Free daycare centers. Free medical and pediatric clinics for anyone who needed it."

"Wow," Cassie said with a shake of her head, impressed. "You really gave it all away to help others?" He nodded and Cassie sighed. "It's hard to believe at the tender age of twenty-one you had that much sensitivity and fore-sight," she said. "Especially considering everything you'd gone through. Most people that age don't even think about the world around them, let alone the people in need in that world." Moved by his unselfish act, Cassie found her defenses crumbling. How very different Beau was from Sofie's father, who'd used his family's wealth to buy more power and political clout so he could terrorize other people. Beau and his family used their money to make the world a better place for others.

Beau was an exceptional, uncommon man who had a

huge heart. What woman wouldn't melt in the face of such absolute kindness and generosity?

Struggling to get her emotions under control Cassie glanced out the window then back at Beau, trying to rein in her emotions as he continued.

"Right now, we're about to break ground on the tenth free clinic in the state. In addition, there's an adjoining daycare center next to each and every one so mothers can get the medical care they need without worrying about who's going to watch their children while they get it."

"And it's all free?" she repeated, having a hard time comprehending this.

He nodded. "Everything." He hesitated a moment. "In fact, in the past two weeks Uncle Jasper and I have been talking about opening up something in Cooper's Cove, something just for kids." Affectionately, he ran a finger down her nose. "And we have Sofie to thank for the idea."

"Sofie?" Cassie repeated, looking at him skeptically. "I'm almost afraid to ask what my daughter's done now."

He chuckled. "Nothing like that, Cass. But you know how interested Sofie is in science?"

"Yeah?"

"Well, Uncle Jasper and I were thinking about starting an after-school club for kids, where they could go to learn about whatever their specific interests are. Science, or math, or biology, or even writing or newspaper work. We figured we'd staff the place with retired experts in their fields, and then ask people in town who are professionals to donate a couple hours a month to the center."

"Beau, that's a fabulous idea, absolutely fabulous. And you can put me down for some hours every month as well."

"There's actually an old storefront building for sale,

right at the end of Main Street, that Uncle Jasper and I have been looking to buy. The club will kill two birds with one stone. It will give kids who have nowhere to go after school a safe, supervised place to spend their time, and it will give their parents some peace of mind, knowing their kids are right in town, safe, and learning something to boot."

Impulsively, Sofie leaned over and gave him a loud, smacking kiss on the mouth.

Blinking in surprise, Beau grinned. "What was that for?" he asked, his lips warmed from hers, and tingling. This was the first time *she'd* actually kissed *him,* and he realized he liked it. "I figure if I know, then I can do it again so I get another kiss."

She kissed him again, then drew back a few inches and looked straight into his eyes. "That's for being the kindest, most generous human being I've ever met." She leaned forward and kissed him again, slower this time, letting her mouth settle over his until they fit together perfectly.

Beau reached for her, dragging her close until her body was pressed along the warm length of his. He tunneled his fingers through the silky strands of her hair, wanting her even closer as he took the kiss deeper.

Cassie moaned, placing her hands on his chest, feeling the warmth of him, the strength of him. In his arms she felt something that had eluded her entire adult life: safety in a man's arms. The feeling that this was right, perfect.

"Hey!" A young police officer rapped on the window, making them jump apart in embarrassment. "No necking in the parking lot. If you want to neck go into the movies like everyone else." The cop paled when Beau turned to look at him. "Oh…uh…Dr. Beau, sorry." The young cop grinned sheepishly. "Thought you were teenagers." He rolled his eyes. "They're always parking in this lot to neck."

"Sorry, Tommy, I was just stealing a kiss from my girl before we took in the matinee."

"Howdy, Ms. Cassie," Tommy said, flashing her a grin and tipping the bill of his cap toward her. She wanted to groan. By this evening everyone in town would know that Tommy Fitzgerald Jr. had caught Dr. Beau and her necking in the parking lot of the movie theater. Cassie wanted to groan.

"Well, I guess I'll be on my way," Tommy said. "You two have a nice day, hear?"

"Thanks, Tommy." Beau turned to her. "Think it's time to go inside?"

"Absolutely," Cassie agreed. "Before half the town shows up to watch the show they think we're going to put on," she added with a laugh.

Grabbing her hand, he pushed open his door and they climbed out.

"Well, Beau, I guess that cinches it then," she said, as they walked across the parking lot toward the theater.

"Cinches what?"

She grinned. "Since you gave away all your money, I guess I'll have to spring for the movie. But next week, it's your turn."

He lifted her hand for a kiss. "Deal."

Chapter Seven

"Listen to me, carefully," Cassie began again, all but gritting her teeth as she spoke carefully through the telephone receiver. "When I ordered those nail-tech tables you guaranteed they'd be delivered by the first of April. Today is Friday, the *thirteenth of April,* and I still don't have my tables." Tempted to simply hang up on the salesman, Cassie tried to rein in her temper. She had a salon full of clients at the moment and didn't want to cause a scene, but still, whatever could go wrong in the past two weeks had. And she was more than just a little frazzled.

Between trying to help Sofie, Brian and Timmy with their science fair project and trying to keep up with the renovations at the salon, she hadn't had time to breathe. And she certainly didn't have time for empty promises from vendors she depended on.

"Yes, I understand perfectly," she said sweetly, keeping her voice low and controlled. "Now you understand. If those tables aren't in my shop by the end of business today, I'm canceling my order. And," she added firmly, "I fully expect a complete refund." Without another word, Cassie slammed down the receiver.

When the phone rang again, Cassie snatched it up with a snarl. "Cassie's Salon and Day Spa," she said into the phone, trying to make her voice pleasant. "May I help you?"

"Yeah, Cass, can you come open the back door?"

"Beau?" Cassie frowned. "Is that you? Where are you? And why do you want me to open the back door?"

"Because Shorty and I are carrying an incredibly heavy nail table and the back door is locked."

"Oh, my God, you've got my tables?" Cassie said with a laugh. "Wait. Wait. I'll be right there." Cassie slammed down the receiver again and dashed through the salon to unlock and open the door.

Beau was standing on the other side with a grin, holding half of what looked like a very heavy table.

"Come in, come in," she said, ushering them inside.

"Ladies," Beau and Shorty both said with a smile as they sailed past the women under the dryer, in aluminum foil, and sitting in the styling chairs.

"How on earth did you get those?" Cassie asked, following. "I just hung up on the salesman who sold those to me. I threatened to cancel the order if they weren't here by end of business today. He told me they hadn't come in from his supplier yet." Cassie put her hands on her hips. "So how did you get them?" she asked with a frown.

"Your mother," Beau said simply, setting the table down for a minute to catch his breath. "Where do you want these?"

Cassie pointed. "Right there, in the empty space right

behind that row of dryers. They should fit perfectly. And how did Mama get my tables when they aren't in from the supplier yet?"

Beau and Shorty proceeded to move the first table into position, pulling off the plastic and taking it with them as they went back outside to get the second table.

"Cassie," Beau all but grunted, "these aren't your tables. At least not the ones you ordered." He set the second table in position, then stood up, pressing a hand to his back. "This morning your mother told Uncle Jasper that the tables you ordered weren't coming."

"But how did Mama—"

Beau held up his hand and grinned. "Maybe we don't really want to know *how* she knew, Cassie," he said, making her laugh. "Anyway, she told Uncle Jasper, who in turn called me at the office and told me. So I asked Shorty to get on the phone and call every beauty supply distributor within a fifty-mile radius."

"Aye, he did," Shorty confirmed with a nod. "Took about ten calls before I found someone who had three in stock. Supplier right outside of Madison as it turns out. I told him to hold them for the Boss, here, and that we'd be in to pick them up sometime this morning."

"Wait a minute," Cassie said, pressing her hand to her forehead. Her headache seemed to be getting worse. "Are you telling me you drove almost a hundred miles round-trip this morning to get these tables for me?"

Shorty looked at Beau and shrugged those massive shoulders. "Did I not make myself clear, Boss?"

Beau laughed and patted his back. "No, you did, Shorty. I think Cassie's just a bit shocked."

Cassie shook her head. "Beau, you're a doctor, not a

delivery man." She pressed her hand to her throbbing forehead, feeling just a tad guilty. "You didn't have to do this," she said, touched beyond measure by his continuous generosity. She didn't think she'd ever known anyone who'd been so supportive of her or her dreams. Beau knew how much this shop meant to her, how hard she worked to earn the right to be a business owner, and he gave her his full and total support. No matter what.

For the first time in her life Cassie realized that she'd met a man she truly could count on and trust.

Shorty was staring at one of Cassie's patrons with a decided frown. "Lassie?" He gave Cassie a nudge. "Are you preparing that one for space travel?" he whispered, giving the woman with aluminum foil wrapped around her hair a nod and making Cassie laugh.

"No, Shorty," she said. "She's having her hair streaked."

"So she's doing that on *purpose?*" he asked, stunned, and Cassie laughed.

"Yes, Shorty. She is," she confirmed as Shorty snuck closer, wanting a better look.

"Cassie, we've got one more table to bring in," Beau said, "but I want to make certain everything's still a go for this afternoon?" He met her gaze and Cassie nodded.

"Sofie's coming here right after school so I can fix her hair. There's no way she can have her picture taken after a day of school without getting her hair combed," she said with a slight frown. "Then you'll pick her up from here and walk her down to Katie's office—"

"With Brian and Timmy," he added and she nodded again.

"Their moms are going to drop the boys off at your office, right?"

"Yeah, right after school. Then I'll take all three kids

over to the newspaper office so Katie can take their picture and interview them." Beau grinned, touching her cheek. "I think it's wonderful of Katie to run an article about some of the kids and their projects in the science fair."

"It's not nepotism, Beau, in spite of how it looks," Cassie assured him with a smile. "Every year the *Cooper's Cove Carrier* runs a feature about the science fair. This year Katie just happened to choose Sofie and her team. But I've got to tell you Sofie was so excited about having her picture in the paper she couldn't sleep last night."

He nodded. "That's understandable. They're all excited about having their pictures and their projects in the newspaper." He frowned slightly. "When Katie's done with the kids, I'll drive them all home."

Cassie sighed, mentally seeing her appointment schedule for today. "I should be home by six at the latest," she said.

He nodded. "Great." He hesitated, not really wanting to leave yet. "If you and Sofie don't have plans for dinner, maybe we can grab something to eat?"

"I'd love to Beau, but Mama and Uncle Jasper have already made plans to take Sofie to a movie." She grinned. "But if you don't have any plans why don't you stay for dinner when you bring Sofie home?"

His face brightened. "Is this a homemade dinner we're talking about?"

She nodded. "Definitely homemade. Last weekend I made a double batch of sauce, two pans of homemade lasagna and my special chicken broth with baby pastina." She rocked back on her heels, aware that half the shop was watching and listening to her. "If I add one of my special salads I'd say that's about as homemade as you can get."

"You've got yourself a deal," Beau said with a grin. "I'm not sure what time Katie will be done with the kids, but as soon as she is, and I get the kids safely home, Sofie and I will be there."

"Sounds like a plan to me." Cassie said, already mentally setting the table, and thinking about any last-minute things she had to pick up at the store on her way home.

"I'll see you tonight, then," Beau said with a nod toward Shorty, letting him know they were ready.

"We'll bring that other table right in, lassie," Shorty said, already heading toward the back door.

She touched his arm. "Beau?"

"Yeah?"

"Thank you." Mindful of all her patrons, Cassie stood on tiptoe and gave him a kiss on the cheek. "For bringing my tables."

"You're welcome. I'll see you later," Beau confirmed as he headed toward the back door. Cassie glanced at the clock. Only six more hours. She sighed, wondering when just being with Beau had become the highlight of her day.

Cassie was nervous as a cat.

She hadn't been this nervous about having a man to dinner at her house in—well, *never* she realized, stunned. It was a new and nerve-racking experience for her. After getting Sofie calmed down from her interview at the news-paper and changed into play clothes so she could go to the movies, Cassie had raced around trying to get everything done.

The kitchen table was set, and although she'd used her mother's good china and linen napkins, it appeared small and homey, rather than romantic and elegant the way the dinner table had been at Beau's.

But she'd done what she could and was just lighting the long, white taper candles when the doorbell rang.

Yanking off her apron, Cassie dropped it on the counter, smoothed her damp, nervous hands down her one good silk dress and shoved her hair back off her face one last time before going to answer the door.

"Wow." Beau stood there, a bouquet of white roses in his hands, staring at her as if he'd never seen her before. She had on a wispy silk dress that might make a blind man weep. It was as black as night and clung to her feminine curves in a way that had his mouth going dry. Although not at all revealing, it had a high neck, long sleeves and a slightly flared skirt that just skimmed her knees, making her long legs look incredibly sexy. She'd pulled her hair back with two black satin barrettes, letting the rest fall like a curtain down her back. "You look beautiful," he all but stammered and she laughed.

"Thank you." She took his arm. "Come in, come in. Dinner is just about ready."

"Here." He handed her the white roses, then watched as emotions claimed her features.

"Oh, Beau, they're beautiful," she said, closing the front door, then lowering her face to smell the fragrant buds. "Absolutely beautiful." She glanced up at him. "How on earth did you know white roses were my favorite?"

He actually flushed a bit. "Let's just say a little bird told me."

She laughed. "And I'll bet that little bird has long brown hair and big brown eyes and favors science, right?"

"I'll never tell," he teased.

"Well, they're beautiful. But I can't even imagine where on earth you got white roses this time of year." The man's thoughtfulness never failed to surprise her.

"We've got a greenhouse on the property. Believe it or not, Shorty is an avid gardener. That man could make dirt grow into something beautiful," he said, inhaling deeply.

"Shorty's a gardener?" she repeated, then shook her head. "You guys are full of surprises," she said with a laugh. "Gardening would be the last thing I'd think Shorty would be interested in."

"The man's got a serious green thumb," he admitted. "As opposed to my thumb, which is black. Everything I try to grow, dies. So Shorty and I made a pact. He'd stay away from my patients as long as I stayed away from his flowers." Beau shrugged. "It's worked out fine." He took another step into the foyer. "Something smells wonderful." Unable to resist, he leaned forward and kissed her. "Besides you," he added, a twinkle in his eye.

Cassie laughed, trying not to be flustered by his easy kiss. She was getting quite used to Beau kissing her. And she had to admit, she liked it. More than she could ever have believed.

"It's dinner. Come on into the kitchen while I finish up some last-minute things and then we can eat."

He followed her into the kitchen, basically following his nose. "I've got to tell you, Cass, I've been looking forward to this all day." He took another deep whiff. "It smells like heaven in here," he said, watching as she stood on tiptoe to try to reach a vase on the top shelf of the cabinet.

"Here, let me do that." He stepped behind her, the warmth of his body brushing the entire length of hers as he reached for the vase. He handed it to her, and their gazes met and held.

Feeling awkward and flustered, Cassie smiled. "Thanks," she said, turning toward the sink to fill the vase with water before arranging the flowers, willing both her heart and her pulse to slow down.

Nervous himself, Beau wandered around the kitchen. "You never told me how on earth you learned to cook?"

She laughed as she stirred the broccoli, garlic and Parmesan cheese that was warming on the stove. "Necessity," she said simply, replacing the cover and turning the gas down to low before turning to him. "Growing up, Mama worked. Even before my father passed away, Mama and Aunt Gracie had the Astrology Parlor." She shrugged, leaning against the counter beside him. Close enough to smell his wonderful masculine scent. Close enough to see the beautiful flecks of gray in his deep blue eyes. Feeling off balance because he was so close and she was feeling so vulnerable, she rubbed her hands up and down her arms. This was the first time they'd been alone together in her house, just the two of them, and she couldn't believe or understand how nervous she was. "Katie and I always chose a project for the summer. And we just sort of decided that one of our projects would be to teach ourselves to cook. That summer we watched every cooking show we could find and checked out so many cookbooks from the library that Ms. Pringle started casting a suspicious eye toward us." Laughing at the memory, Cassie shook her head. "We cooked all day, every day. Making mistake after mistake. But learning an awful lot in the process." Cassie shrugged. "Neither Katie nor I ever liked fast food so cooking seemed like a viable alternative."

"You're kidding?" Beau said, surprised. "I thought everyone loved fast food?" He grinned. "Personally, I'm a Twinkies man. I consider it one of the four basic food groups."

She laughed. "I don't think I've ever eaten a Twinkie," she admitted, making his eyes widen.

"You've never eaten a Twinkie?" he repeated, truly shocked and she laughed.

"Uh, no. I wouldn't kid about something like that." She shrugged as she reached for the bottle of red wine and opened it. "I neglected to mention that in addition to not liking fast food, I'm not really fond of sweets, either." He took the bottle from her, their fingers brushing, and filled the wine glasses on the table, then picked hers up and handed it to her.

"You poor thing, have you seen a doctor about this?" he inquired, his face serious, his eyes mischievous. She took a sip of her wine, refrained, just barely, from making a face and shook her head.

"No, I haven't," she admitted, taking another sip of her wine, and this time, unable to resist making a face.

"I take it you're not fond of wine, either?" he said with a lift of his brow and she shook her head again.

"Actually it gives me a whopping headache. But what's lasagna without red wine?"

"Headache free?" he answered as he took the glass from her and set it on the counter along with his own. He opened the refrigerator and extracted two cold bottles of water. "Now this—this is the drink of champions. And no calories," he added with a wiggle of his brow, handing her the bottle of water. "Now, what were we talking about. Oh yeah, your cooking. You really do enjoy cooking, don't you?"

She smiled. "Love it, always have," she admitted. "Although when Sofie and I were living in Madison I didn't have much time to cook. I did most of it on the weekends, then froze things so when I got home from work I could grab something and pop it in the oven. That way we'd have a homemade dinner every night."

He smiled at her, impressed. "You are a seriously organized person, Cass, you know that don't you?"

She laughed. "Yeah, so I've been told." She frowned slightly. "I don't think I'm going to be able to pass on my love of cooking to Sofie, though. She's more interested in cooking up scientific formulas as opposed to spaghetti sauce."

He chuckled. "They each have their merits." He caught her chin in his hand. It was a mistake to look at him, Cassie realized, because she always found herself drowning in the depths of his beautiful eyes. "You're not nervous, are you?" he asked quietly, and instinctively she laid a hand to his chest. She could feel the warm, steady beat of his heart through his shirt, reminding her he was a virile, dangerous male.

Her mouth went dry, and she licked her lips. The movement of his gaze followed her tongue, only making her more nervous and self-conscious.

"Beau, I…I don't have a lot of experience with this male-female stuff." Which was probably why she always looked at him and wondered how he could make her feel so many traitorous things she'd promised herself she'd never again let herself feel.

"No experience necessary to have dinner with a friend, Cass," he assured her, his gaze traveling over her facial features. "I think you can handle that, can't you?" His gaze searched hers and she nodded mutely.

"I guess so," she admitted with a sigh.

"Good." He set his water down on the counter and slid his arms around her waist. "I've been thinking about kissing you again for…weeks," he admitted, and her pulse leapt like a frog in flight.

"I…" He pressed a finger to her mouth.

"Don't get nervous, Cass," he said quietly, his gaze on her mouth. "I'm not going to hurt you. I'd never hurt you."

As he lowered his mouth to hers, she wanted to believe him, longed to believe him. She wound her arms greedily around him and leaned into him, needing to feel the warmth of him as he took the kiss deeper, and she knew that she was already in trouble.

With a soft moan, she pressed closer, wanting this kiss to go on forever, wanting these wonderful feelings and sensations to stay with her forever. But no matter what she felt, no matter what Beau made her feel, she couldn't ever forget that Sofie came first.

Always.

Like it or not, she was going to have to rein in her feelings and put them in their proper perspective. She couldn't afford to be hurt, and more importantly, she couldn't afford to risk having her precious daughter hurt.

With another soft murmur, Cassie reluctantly pulled back as the oven buzzer went off, signaling the lasagna was ready.

Slowly, Beau drew back as well, his eyes glazed, his mouth slightly swollen from their kiss. He gave her waist an affectionate squeeze before stepping away. Dragging a hand through his hair, he reached for his bottle of water and took a long drink.

Cassie watched him for a moment, her heart hammering in her chest and realized that somehow, someway, when she wasn't looking, her feelings for Beau had changed. Somewhere along the line she'd fallen in love with him. And for the life of her, she had no idea what she was going to do about it.

Chapter Eight

The following Wednesday morning, Cassie was surprised to find Beau waiting outside her shop when she arrived to open up.

"Beau, what are you doing here?"

"Uh, Cassie," Beau said nervously. "I know we're supposed to go to the matinee this afternoon, but I was wondering if you'd mind if we played hooky and did something else." He couldn't contain his grin. "There's something I want to show you."

She chuckled as she opened the shop door and let them both in. "Okay, so we're going to play hooky from hooky, is that it?"

For the past several weeks, she'd deliberately not booked any Wednesday afternoon appointments so she could have the time free.

They'd gone to a matinee every week since that first Wednesday and it had fast become the highlight of Cassie's week. For a few hours she had adult companionship and some time alone with Beau. They'd spent hours talking about everything and anything, including the movies they'd been seeing.

Beau nodded. "Yep, and there's a fabulous dinner at Carm's at the end of the day if you agree."

"Okay, I'm sold. I love Carm's food." She stuck out her hand. "It's a deal."

He shook her hand. "Okay, I'll meet you at my office at two."

"This?" Cassie said nervously, glancing at Beau who was standing on the sidewalk grinning like a loon as he looked at the empty building in front of them. "This is what you wanted to show me?"

The building looked abandoned, and had apparently been empty for quite a while since the windows were filthy, and a few were even cracked. The wood along the bottom of the green front door was rotting away and several chunks had already broken through to the other side. There must have been a sign overhead at one time, but all that was left now was a few metal rings that had probably held the sign in place.

"This is what you wanted to show me?" Cassie asked again, turning back to Beau and trying not to frown.

"Yep, isn't it great?" he asked, digging in his pants pocket for the key. He stepped forward and unlocked the door, using his body weight to push it open. "Be careful," he said, glancing behind him as he entered. "Some of the floorboards are loose."

Gingerly, Cassie followed him inside, mindful of where she walked. Dust motes floated through the stale, stagnant air, and she had to hold her nose to keep back a sneeze. When a board creaked and moved under her foot, she reached for the back of Beau's shirt, fearing she might lose her balance or worse, fall through the loose floorboards. He reached behind him and grabbed her hand, holding it tightly in his.

"This, Cassie, is the new official headquarters of the Cooper's Cove Kids Club, an afternoon learning facility for anyone and everyone in town." He walked deeper into the building, still holding her hand. "We've got about three thousand square feet total, and I've already got architects drawing up the plans for the renovations. I thought we'd simply divide it up into what I like to call lab rooms. Each room will be for a different subject. One for science, one for math, one for writing, cooking, anything the kids are interested in." He tugged her hand, bringing her closer. "I know it doesn't look like much now, but give me a couple of months and it will be fabulous. I've already got commitments from most of the professionals in town to donate a few hours every month, including your aunt Louella, who's going to teach astrology. Uncle Jasper's going to teach chemistry, Katie offered to come in as soon as the baby is born and teach about the newspaper business, and even Lucas volunteered to teach the kids about law enforcement." Beau was grinning like a Cheshire cat, his excitement almost palpable. "Everyone's just been great with their time, Cass, including Mayor Hannity, who's offered to come in and talk politics."

"If anyone understands politics, it's the mayor," she said with a laugh. "Since he's been the mayor for as long as anyone can remember." She glanced around, trying to see what Beau was seeing—not an abandoned, run-down office building, but a clubhouse for kids. "Well, as I said before, put me down for a few hours a month as well. I'm not sure how many kids are interested in cosmetology, but hey, I'm willing to teach if they're willing to learn."

"Thanks, Cass, that means a lot to me, especially considering how busy you are." Beau looked a little sheepish as he tugged her close again, wrapping his arms around her waist. "I've got a confession to make."

"A confession?" she repeated, glancing up at him and trying not to smile. "I can't wait to hear this," she said with a grin. "Okay, shoot."

"I have an ulterior motive for inviting you to Carm's for dinner tonight," he said, still looking sheepish. She drew back and pretended to look stunned.

"No. An ulterior motive for inviting me to the best, and only, sitdown restaurant in Cooper's Cove?" She pressed her hands to his chest. Her heart was doing a slow free fall because he was so close. "And what could that ulterior motive be?"

"I want to ask Carm if either he or his daughter would volunteer a few hours at the club each month to teach cooking classes and maybe even conduct cooking demonstrations. I thought it would be great if every couple of months the kids showed off the skills they learned by having an all day Kid-Club Festival."

"That's a fabulous idea, Beau."

"I've even got Mrs. Cushing to come in and teach violin twice a week, too."

"She's been teaching violin forever and the kids all love her." Cassie laughed suddenly. "Did you ever take lessons from her as a kid?"

Beau shook his head. "Afraid not, Cass." He wiggled

his fingers at her. "In spite of the fact that I'm a doctor, I'm all thumbs when it comes to music."

She chuckled. "You're not the only one. Katie and I both took violin lessons—for one week before poor Mrs. Cushing had to tell our mothers that we couldn't carry a tune if she gave us an empty wheelbarrow."

Cassie glanced around the dirty, dank space. She could see it now, as Beau did—the labs, the kids, the projects— and her heart swelled when she realized how much he truly cared about others, especially kids.

It was so difficult for her to reconcile Beau's attitude toward life and children with what she'd experienced with Sofie's father.

Stephen Caldwell had been a self-centered man-child who used his money as a weapon against people and who didn't even have enough compassion in his heart to care about his own child.

Yet Beau, who had no children but just as much if not more money than the Caldwells, used his wealth to improve the life of children he didn't even know.

It was a stark contrast in personalities and Cassie couldn't help but wonder what her life and Sofie's would have been like if she'd fallen hopelessly in love with Beau at the age of seventeen instead of someone like Stephen?

"Ready to see the rest?" Beau asked and she nodded.

"Just lead the way."

Carm's was, technically, an Italian restaurant, but they also served the only and best steaks in town. Run by Carmen Santini, a widower, and his daughter, Gina, they served authentic made-from-scratch Italian dishes as well as prime steaks and chops.

Carm greeted Beau warmly. "Doc, Doc, it's been too long," Carm complained with a smile as he led them to a private booth. Almost sixty, he was a small, stocky man with a shock of silver hair, and a face aged by life and the sun. "It's good to see you again, Doc," Carm said as he handed them menus. "Anything you want, I'll make it special," he promised with a wink. "Let me get you a glass of wine to whet your palate."

"Carm, would you mind making it bottled water?" Beau asked, mindful of Cassie's palate.

"No, no, of course not. Whatever you like." Carm hurried off and Beau turned all his attention to Cassie.

"Another friend?" Cassie asked with a smile as she picked up her menu. She hadn't had a bite of food since breakfast and realized she was famished.

Beau sighed, setting his menu down without even looking at it. "Everybody's a friend in Cooper's Cove," he said. He nodded toward her menu. "Any idea what you'd like?"

"I honestly don't know. Everything looks wonderful."

"If you're in the mood for Italian, try the spinach lasagna. Gina makes it fresh every morning with Carm's homemade sauce. Although maybe you're the wrong person to recommend it to."

"Why?"

"Because your spinach lasagna was to die for, and I don't know that Gina's can stand up to yours."

"Well, just because I make my own doesn't preclude me from enjoying or appreciating someone else's."

"If you'd rather have a steak, the T-bone can't be beat."

"And what are you having?"

"A steak." He pressed his fingers to his tired eyes for a

moment. "I think my body needs some protein right about now. I've been running on fumes for several days."

"I'll have the same, then." Inherently needing to comfort others, Cassie laid her hand over his. "Beau, are you sure you're not taking on too much," she asked quietly as Carm set their bottled water in front of them and quickly took their orders. "You're helping the kids with their science project. You're running your practice. And now you're trying to get a building renovated to start a club for kids. That's an awful lot to have on your plate."

"Maybe it is a lot," he admitted. "But I'm enjoying it, every single moment of every part." He smiled. "The kids have been great, Cass, just wonderful. And it's only a few more weeks until the science fair, so once that's over I'll have a little bit more free time."

"Beau," Cassie said carefully. "I don't know how to thank you for all the time and attention and patience you've showered on Sofie."

He grinned, sipped his water, then slid his hand along the back of the booth so he could touch the silkiness of her hair. "She's a fabulous little girl, Cassie. I've told you that," he said, meeting her gaze.

"I know, but she's really never had anyone, at least not a male anyone, give her so much time and attention."

"What about her father?" he asked quietly, watching her carefully. "Cassie?" His fingers toyed with the silky ends of her hair. "Will you tell me about Sofie's father?"

"Her…father?" Cassie stammered and he nodded.

"Do you mind?"

She thought about it for a moment. For some reason, now that she'd gotten to know Beau so well, gotten to know the kind of man he truly was, she had no hesitancy telling him about Sofie's father.

"I usually don't talk about him," she admitted. "But if you really want to know…" Nervous, she lifted her water to wet her suddenly dry lips.

"I do, Cass, I really do."

"You know how everyone at Cooper's Cove High School has to do a community service project for a summer in order to graduate?"

He smiled. "Yeah, I did a whole summer of volunteer work at the town nursing home." He made a face. "Geriatrics. Taught me kids and babies were definitely more my speed."

"Yeah, well, I volunteered at the youth camp for handicapped children, the one on the other side of the lake. I'd always loved kids and I thought it would be fun." She hesitated before going on. "Sofie's father, his name is Stephen Caldwell—"

"Wait a minute," Beau said with a frown, trying to place that name. "Caldwell. Why do I know that name?"

She chuckled, but the sound held no mirth. "You know it because his father is a very prominent former senator from Wisconsin, and the Caldwells are one of the wealthiest, most prominent families in the state. Sort of the Midwestern version of the Kennedys. Stephen lived during the summers in that big secluded fishing lodge on the other side of Cooper's Cove Lake. His family still owns it I believe."

"Ah," he said with a nod of acknowledgment. "Now I know who he is, or rather who his family is."

"Yeah, well, I didn't, not really, since I never hung around with the so-called 'rich crowd.' I thought Stephen had volunteered at the camp because he loved children. It turned out his father had sent him to camp to keep him out of trouble and get him out of another scrape, but of course, I didn't know that at the time."

"What kind of a scrape, Cassie?"

"I don't know. All I know is that whatever it was, his father had bailed him out. Something his father apparently had a great deal of practice doing. Stephen got into trouble, his father bought off the problem and made it disappear. Anyway, by the time I met Stephen he could lie with a straight face like no one I've ever known. Of course I was so young and inexperienced at the time I didn't realize he was lying to me."

"You thought he loved you?" Beau asked gently and she nodded, telling herself she wouldn't cry. She wouldn't be embarrassed at her own stupidity. She'd gotten her precious daughter out of the fiasco and that was worth more than anything else.

"Yeah," she said with a soft sniffle and a sigh. "I really thought he loved me and we were going to have the very traditional happily ever after. He was very convincing," she admitted with a sad smile. "Charming, gorgeous, and just…a real practiced Romeo at seventeen." She shook her head, unable to believe Stephen had been that good. Or that she'd been that naive. "I fell head over heart for his 'happily ever after' story of how we'd find ways to be together during the school year and then get married after graduation and have these fabulous careers and life."

"But you got pregnant?" he guessed and she nodded.

"Bingo." She smiled at him, surprised to see not distaste or disapproval in his eyes, but sympathy and compassion.

"The 'happily-ever-after' scenario lasted just until I told Stephen I was pregnant."

"What happened, Cass?" Beau asked quietly.

She had to take another sip of water and a deep breath, surprised it still stung after all this time. Not because of her feelings for Stephen—those had been killed long ago—but because it hurt to know that Stephen had thrown away Sofie, the best thing that could have ever happened to him.

"He told his parents. I was invited to the Caldwells' lodge to discuss…my situation."

"*Your* situation," Beau repeated with some heat. "You didn't exactly get in that 'situation' all on your own."

"True, but that wasn't important to the Caldwells. All that was important to them was protecting Stephen and the family name. Stephen's dad has been grooming him since birth to take over his political empire. Having a pregnant young wife from 'the wrong side of town,' with a mother who was a psychic and an aunt who ran an astrology parlor, well, my goodness, what on earth would people think?"

"*Think?*" Beau repeated, appalled. "Their son was acting like an ass and all they cared about was what people thought?"

"Oh, wait, there's more. The Caldwells made it clear that they were indeed going to help with 'my little problem' as they continually referred to Sofie. They offered me a large sum of money, a very *large* sum of money, to get rid of the problem."

"Oh, Lord," Beau muttered with a shake of his head. "These people didn't know you very well, did they?"

"They didn't know me at all," she said with some heat.

"You turned them down?" he asked mildly and she

nodded, making him smile. "Probably told them what they could do with their money as well, didn't you?"

She laughed because it was clear Beau knew her much better than Stephen ever had. "You're right," she said with a sigh, running a finger over the rim of her water glass. "But then things got *really* ugly."

"There's more of this nonsense from these horrible people?"

"Oh, I'm just getting started. When they realized I wasn't for sale, and neither was my child, the Caldwells basically told me that they were completely disavowing any knowledge of me or my problem."

"You mean Sofie?"

"Yeah. For a while I swear I thought I was going to have to name the kid 'Problem' just because that's the only way the Caldwells ever referred to her. Anyway, Senator Caldwell came right out and told me that unless I signed this document denying any possibility of Stephen's paternity, he would call the police and tell them I had tried to 'shake him down' for money, and I'd be arrested, disgraced…yada, yada, yada. As an added bonus, he said he'd pay twenty of Stephen's friends to all say they could have been the father of my child thereby proving that I was not just a slut, but a greedy, devious slut."

Horrified, Beau dropped his arm from the back of the booth, to her shoulders and pulled her closer. "My God, Cassie, these people are…animals."

"You think?" she asked with a shaky smile, realizing that it felt good to tell someone about this. To tell Beau about it. She'd instinctively known he would understand. "Anyway, I told Senator Caldwell that I'd be happy to sign anything he wanted. But I wanted something in return."

Beau looked at her for a long moment and then he grinned and shook his head. "He thought you wanted more money, didn't he?"

"Yep," she said with a nod. "He thought I wanted to up the ante, so to speak."

He chuckled. "But you didn't, did you?"

"Nope, I didn't want a dime, not one thin dime. I didn't want nor would I ever take a penny from those people. What I wanted was something far more valuable and important. I wanted a guarantee that those horrible people would never ever have any contact with my child. They may not have wanted Sofie, but I did. And right from the beginning, Beau, she was mine. All mine. And I wouldn't give her up or get rid of her for any amount of money. What I wanted, in return for my signature stating that Stephen was not Sofie's father, was Senator Caldwell's signature on a document stating that neither he, nor anyone in his family, would *ever* try to contact me or my child in any way ever again."

"So you were trying to protect Sofie even before she was born?" Beau said softly, understanding immediately.

"I didn't care what they did to me, Beau, I truly didn't. They embarrassed and humiliated me and threatened to sully my reputation and have me charged with a criminal offense." She shook her head, frightened after all this time by the mere thought of what they'd tried to do to her. "And all I'd done was made the mistake of falling in love with their idiot son." Cassie shook her head and Beau lifted a hand to wipe an errant tear from her cheek. "I knew if I did nothing else I had to protect my child from these people. I didn't ever want my child to be at risk because I had such damn poor judgment when it came to men."

She waited as Carm set down their salads. "All I wanted was to get as far and as fast away from those people as possible. One hot day at the end of August, I met Senator Caldwell at his attorney's office. He'd already had the papers drawn up, two copies of each, and I signed both of them as did he." Lost in the memory, Cassie absently picked up her fork and pushed a few bits of her salad around on her plate. "Before I left that day, Senator Caldwell warned me that if I ever did anything to embarrass him or his family, if I ever tried to 'come back to the well' so to speak, hoping to dip into it for financial gain, or ever mentioned his son in connection with my 'bastard child' he'd ruin me." Now the tears came faster. "I'm embarrassed to admit he scared the living daylights out of me, Beau. I was barely seventeen years old and hadn't even told my mother I was pregnant yet."

"Oh, Lord, Cassie, you dealt with these people all on your own?" Beau's admiration for her grew by leaps and bounds. He couldn't believe she'd actually stood up to these people at the tender age of seventeen. She had guts, courage and, more than anything else, integrity, something no amount of money could buy.

"I figured I was old enough to get myself into the mess, I'd better be old enough to get myself out. So, yeah, I dealt with them on my own." She took a deep breath and a sip of water. "When I finally told Mama, she was just so wonderful, Beau, and so supportive." Now her tears welled in earnest, and she quickly dabbed at them with her napkin. "Never once did she fault me or my judgment. Never once did she make me feel ashamed or embarrassed. And she's loved, accepted and adored Sofie from the moment she was born."

"Naturally. That's your mother's nature, Cassie." He

smiled at her. "And the apple doesn't fall far from the tree." He lifted her hand and kissed it. "You're not the first young girl to fall in love with the wrong man, Cassie. I think you're a little too hard on yourself. When we're young we have a tendency to lead with our hearts instead of thinking with our heads."

"I agree with you, there, but at the time, it sure felt like I was the only idiot female in the world."

He nodded, understanding completely. "So what happened after you got rid of the Caldwells?"

"I started my senior year of high school almost two months pregnant. I hadn't told anyone, except Mama, Aunt Louella and Katie, so when I really started to show, I dropped out of school. Afterward, I went back and got my GED. Mama wanted us to live with her—to stay with her, but I was young and stubborn. At the time I felt her offer was an easy way out for me, and it hit too close to home. I wanted to be a mature, responsible parent for my daughter's sake. And I felt if I stayed with Mama, I wouldn't be any better than Stephen because I let my mother bail me out."

It sounded so much like her he had to smile. "None of this surprises me," he said, kissing her hand again.

"I didn't want my daughter to think her mother was irresponsible. So I applied for and received a scholarship to a beauty school in Madison. Sofie and I moved and I found a wonderful caretaker for Sofie during the day while I was at school. At night, I found a job—cleaning office buildings—where I could take Sofie with me." She shrugged. "I did that until she was almost three. By then I had graduated and started working in a salon in Madison. I stayed there, trying to build up my clientele until Aunt Louella got married a few months ago. I came home for the wedding and the opportunity to buy the salon came up. I knew I couldn't pass it up. It was time to come home, Beau. I missed Mama. I missed Cooper's Cove. And most of all I missed having the kind of childhood for my daughter that I'd had. I wanted all of that for her, and that's why I'm here."

"What about Caldwell, Cass? Have you ever heard from any of them?"

She shook her head. "Nope, not a word, although his family still uses the lodge, or so I've heard. They've kept their promise and so did I."

"So what you're telling me is this man just gave up his own flesh and blood because his father was afraid of how it would look?"

"You got it."

Beau shook his head. Now he understood why Cassie was so skittish around men, and why she'd never trusted her judgment enough to get involved with another one.

"Here we go, Dr. Beau." Carmen approached and set down two steaming silver charger plates sizzling with steak. Next to them, he set down two double-baked potatoes, oozing with melted cheese.

Cassie took one sniff and almost swooned.

"Enjoy, enjoy," Carmen instructed with a smile. "And Ms. Cassie, we all saw the newspaper article yesterday about little Sofie and her science fair project." Carmen put his hands on his heart. "Such a beauty. And so smart. You must be very, very proud of her?"

Cassie had to swallow the lump in her throat, knowing that even strangers appeared to care more about Sofie than her own father ever had. "Oh, Carm, I am, I truly am. Thank you."

"You're very welcome." Carm started to back away. "Enjoy your dinner."

* * *

By the time they'd finished dinner, dessert and coffee, it was almost ten. Cassie realized they'd been talking almost nonstop for three hours, or rather she'd been talking nonstop for most of that time. Somehow Beau had managed to break through the ice around her heart until she actually felt comfortable enough to tell him anything.

"You know, Cass," he said as he sipped his coffee, "you're not the only one who has poor judgment when it comes to the opposite sex."

"What do you mean?" She turned to face him. Relaxed and tired, she snuggled against the booth.

"Do you remember the day you asked me if I had ever thought about getting married, and I said once, but then added some nonsense about having a cold heart?" He glanced at her. She was watching him—listening to him intently.

"I remember," she said quietly.

Beau sighed. "I was engaged once, in med school," he admitted with another sigh. "I was head over heels in love. First love," he corrected with a shake of his head. "It's always the worst."

"What happened?"

He realized that until this moment he'd never told anyone this story, fearing it would embarrass him. But now, with Cassie, he had no fear of embarrassment, only a need to share.

"I overheard her bragging to some of her girlfriends about how she'd bagged the Bradford heir."

"Oh, my God," Cassie said, nearly splashing her coffee over the rim of her cup. "That's how she referred to you?"

He laughed but the sound held no humor. "Apparently that's how just about everyone referred to me. Miraculously, I was no longer Fatty Four-Eyes. Now, I was merely a bank account. In that instant, I guess I realized for the first time that no one really valued me for who or what I was, but merely for what I had."

"Oh, Beau." Cassie laid her hand on his arm, her heart aching. "I'm sorry. That's just so cruel I can't even begin to comprehend such a thing. You're worth more than your…worth," she said quietly, meaning it. "And unfortunately those horrid people never learned that a person's worth isn't *in their* worth, either."

"I broke off the engagement the same day," he said, reaching for her hand and cradling it in his own. "And I never looked back."

"And never took another chance?"

"No." Beau sighed. "Remember the day I told you about my childhood?"

"I remember." It was burned into her memory, and every time she thought about it her heart ached.

"Remember when I said the kids who do the bullying forget their actions, but the one who is bullied suffers the effects for a very long time?"

Cassie nodded.

"That day, the day I heard her bragging, I've got to tell you, Cass, Fatty Four-Eyes felt like he was back. I mean it struck me that if I didn't have a fortune how would people really see me?"

Cassie nodded, understanding so much more about him now. No wonder he was constantly dodging the fortune hunters his uncle sicced on him. He already knew in advance what kind of women they were: they wanted to meet him just *because* he had money.

Cretins, all of them, she decided.

"So you meant that the wedding didn't come off because of her cold heart, right?" Cassie asked, and he nodded.

"Yeah. You know, Cass, for a long while I simply couldn't get my mind around the concept that women didn't look at me as a person—but as a meal ticket."

"Oh, Beau, not all women are that way."

"I know, Cassie, I know," he said, brushing a wayward strand of hair from her cheek, and letting his thumb linger to caress the silky skin. "You're not that way."

Cassie was one of those rare woman who couldn't care less what he had or how much he was worth. She was the kind of woman who judged a man on his character, his actions, his morals and his integrity. And he had a feeling money never even entered her thought process.

"I was really broken up for a while," he admitted with a sheepish smile. "Primarily because I felt foolish. And stupid. And more than a little embarrassed. And it bruised the old male ego for quite a while as well. But like I said, quite frankly it simply had never occurred to me that some-one—anyone—would marry for money. I mean, when you think about it, it's downright ludicrous," he said with a laugh. "How could you settle for something so cold and intangible as money, rather than the other half of your soul? The person you were destined to be with. And how do you live with yourself if you do?"

"Sounds like a devil's bargain to me," Cassie said quietly, just watching him, enjoying his touch.

The lights from the table candle glinted off his features. She couldn't look at his mouth without thinking about the way it made her feel, without wanting it on her own. Suddenly nervous, Cassie deliberately averted her gaze, glancing away, fearing if she didn't, she just might jump him.

"How could someone trade away the love of their life for mere money? I just don't understand it, Cass."

"Any more than I understand how someone could simply walk away from their own flesh and blood," she said, wanting him to know she understood completely.

"I'm sorry you never met my parents, Cass, I think you would have liked them. A lot. Although I was only five when they died, I remember so much about them. You couldn't be in a room with the two of them without feeling how much in love they were." He shrugged. "I guess I always imagined and expected to have what my parents had."

"There's nothing wrong with wanting that, Beau," Cassie said, realizing he'd voiced thoughts secretly buried in his heart, the same as she had. Secrets she'd never shared with anyone.

"Cass, my parents not only had a deep, true love but a meeting of the minds as well. My dad was brilliant, just like Uncle Jasper, but my mom was no slouch in the brains department, either, and could hold her own against anyone, including my dad." He chuckled suddenly. "I have to tell you something that tickled me to no end. Since I was too young to really remember too many details about my folks, Uncle Jasper made sure to tell me stories about them so that I never forgot them."

"That's an incredibly loving, sweet thing to do," she said, wishing she'd gotten to know Beau's parents.

"Well, apparently when my mom and dad met, they were both in graduate school. Starving students, as my dad used to say. About a month after they met, they eloped. Uncle Jasper swears that when they eloped, my mother hadn't a clue who my dad really was or that he even had money. Like Uncle Jasper, my father was brilliant, eccentric and terribly absentminded and forgetful. He was always losing his wallet, or leaving it somewhere so my mother ended up paying for everything, including their marriage license the day they got married. Apparently my mother teased my dad that she was perfectly happy to marry a starving, struggling scientist even if it meant she was probably going to have to support them both until they were old and gray."

"Uh-oh," Cassie said with a laugh. "What happened when she found out the truth?"

"You mean that my dad wasn't a starving struggling scientist, but one of only two living heirs to the Bradford Plastics fortune?"

Cassie nodded. "Yep, that would be the truth I was talking about."

Beau laughed. "Uncle Jasper said my dad feared he was going to have the shortest marriage in history because my mother was furious, absolutely furious, when he told her the truth. Uncle Jasper swears it's the first and only time he ever saw my mother speechless."

"Sounds like Uncle Jasper adored your mother."

"Oh, he did, and from what I gathered, she adored him. When she finally learned the truth about my dad's situation, apparently she was utterly terrified all that money would change things—their relationship, their life—something my poor dad just didn't understand." Beau shook his head. "My dad actually said to her with a perfectly straight face, 'This changes nothing, Bess, unless you expect *me* to start paying for our dates now that you think I've a spot of money?'" Beau laughed and shook his head. "She hit him in the head with a pillow and told him they were never to speak of the dreaded Bradford money again. And as far as I know, they never did. They were happily and madly in love until the day they died—together."

"Oh, Beau," Cassie said softly, reversing roles on him and lifting his hand to her mouth for a comforting kiss. "They sound wonderful, and I'm so sorry they were taken from you so early. From the sound of it, they were very much in love and loved you very much."

"Yep to both, so you can imagine how I felt when I learned my fiancée was interested only in the Bradford fortune and not at all in the Bradford person."

"Oh, absolutely," she agreed. "But she was an idiot, Beau. To look at you and see only your fortune...." Cassie's voice trailed off for a moment as she tried to think of something comparable. "Well, that's like looking at Uncle Jasper and only seeing—"

"An eccentric?" he supplied for her and she laughed because he did truly understand.

"Yeah. Only seeing an eccentric when there's so much more to him, so many layers and facets, and each and every one of them kind, gentle and good." She hesitated for a moment, glancing down at her hands, then back up at him. "Beau, I have a confession to make and it's a bit embarrassing."

"Uh-oh," he said with a smile, lifting her chin so she'd be forced to look at him. "Come on, Cass, after everything we've talked about tonight you shouldn't be embarrassed to tell me anything."

"You're right," she said, taking a breath for courage. "I'll admit that when I first met you I didn't like you or trust you simply because you had money."

"No!" Beau drew back and feigned shock. "I'd never have known," he teased and she smiled.

"Was I that bad?"

"Well, at your aunt Louella's wedding my body temperature probably dropped ten degrees just from the chill radiating off you." Laughing, he shook his head. "And since that's not normally the reaction I get from women I was stumped and couldn't figure out what on earth I'd ever done to you, especially since I didn't really know you."

"It wasn't you, personally, Beau," she assured him with a smile. "It was just…I'd heard all the rumors about you being a womanizer," she said, and he groaned loudly. "Not to mention the fact that the only other thing people talked about was…"

"Wait, let me guess, the Bradford fortune?" he said, wincing when she nodded.

She shrugged. "So I just assumed you were rich, rotten and clearly cut from the same soiled, spoiled cloth as Stephen."

"No wonder you wanted no part of me, considering your experiences with Stephen and his selfish family." Beau cupped her cheek in his hand and she saw so many things in his eyes, things that stirred her frightened heart and made that peculiar yearning begin in the deepest part of her, the part she hid from everyone. "Do you still think I'm like Stephen, Cass?"

"No, Beau, not at all. I've taken the time to look below the surface to all the layers beneath." She smiled sleepily at him, nestling against the warmth of his hand. "Now I know you're so much more than what gossips think or say you are. And the only thing you have in common with Stephen is you're from the same species—I think," she added with a delicate frown, making him chuckle again.

"Beau, I truly do think you're one of the kindest, most generous men I've ever met. And my idea of generous doesn't have anything to do with money or wealth, but everything to do with being a truly good human being." Stunned by her admission, Cassie tried to backpedal, her heart pounding in trepidation when she realized what she'd just said. She wasn't accustomed to expressing her feelings for a man—probably because she wasn't accustomed to *allowing* herself to have feelings for a man. "And probably the best friend I've ever had," she quickly added, seeing his eyes dim just a bit.

She had to say it, had to get the words out, had to put things into perspective for both their sakes.

Beau had made it clear they were *just* friends, and that he wasn't interested in anything more, and neither was she, she told herself. So there was no sense letting her heart or her imagination get away with her just because they'd shared a few kisses, a few secrets, a few life-altering moments. No point in her thinking there was something more here than there was. That was a good way for her to get her heart broken again. And she was too smart for that, wasn't she?

"Well, Cassie, at the risk of being redundant, I feel the same way about you." Before he could think about it, he leaned across the booth and gently brushed his lips lightly across hers. "Thanks for a terrific evening."

"Thank you," she said, her heart fluttering. "For dinner and for trusting me enough to tell me about your past and even your parents."

"And thank you for trusting me enough to tell me about Stephen." He glanced down at their joined hands. "It means a lot to me, Cassie, your trust. It's not something I take lightly."

"I know," she said quietly, giving his hand a squeeze. "It's not something I give lightly, either."

"Maybe that's why it's so important to me." He kissed her hand again. "Ready to go?"

She nodded, following him as he slid out of the booth and realizing that she did indeed trust Beau in a way she'd never trusted another man.

Chapter Nine

When the salon phone rang shortly after six the next evening, Cassie was still sitting at the reception desk, trying to catch up on paperwork.

"Cassie's Salon and Day Spa," she said automatically, still tallying figures. She'd closed for the day and turned off most of the lights. The ones in front of the shop, and over the front door and desk offered plenty of light so she could work. It was a little eerie, but peaceful and perfect for her to concentrate on her paperwork.

"You're still at the salon," Beau said and Cassie sighed, rubbing her throbbing forehead.

"I'm doing paperwork," she said absently. "I'm so far behind, Beau. We've been so busy I just haven't been able to keep up." Cassie sighed, opened a drawer and rummaged around for some aspirin. "If I don't get caught up tonight, I can't start the inventory this weekend, and I have to have that done before the end of the month so I know exactly what supplies I need to reorder to make certain I'm prepared for the rush next month."

"I hear you, Cass."

"Where are you?" she asked with a frown.

"At your house."

"*My* house?" Cassie thought for a moment, then dawning horror made her groan. "Oh, God, Beau, I forgot, didn't I?" She sighed, resting her aching forehead in her hand. "Tonight's the night the kids are putting the papier-mâché replica of the solar system together, right?"

"Right."

"Oh, Lord, and I promised Sofie I'd be there to help." Cassie glanced at the stack of paperwork she still had to do. "Beau, I'm sorry. I really did forget, I truly did. I just got so busy today I haven't even had a moment to think."

"Or eat, I'll bet."

"No, not that, either," she said, realizing that was probably why her head throbbed. "Let me just finish what I'm doing and I can be home in half an hour."

"Cassie, I have a better idea. I'll pitch in for you with the kids, so you don't have to worry about it. And before you protest, let me add that when they find out we're going to order pizza for dinner I'm sure they'll be thrilled and won't even realize you're not here. Your mom and Uncle Jasper are both here as well and you know they'll pitch in and help. I'm also going to call Carm's and have him send something over for you to eat. That way you can work as late as you like—without that headache," he added, surprising her.

"How did you know I had a headache?" she asked with a smile.

"Hey, I'm a doctor, remember? And if you haven't eaten

all day and you've been as busy and stressed as you were this morning when I saw you, you're bound to have a head-ache."

"I…I don't know what to say, Beau. How to thank you." Cassie closed her eyes. Her feelings for Beau had grown by leaps and bounds, day by day. And he was so good with Sofie, he couldn't have treated her better if she'd been his own.

Cassie knew she was in way over her head. What she felt for Beau was not something she'd ever felt before. It was wonderful and the only word that came to mind was…natural. With Beau she felt as if she'd finally found where she belonged. Oh yeah, she thought, she was in way over her head with no idea what to do about it.

"No thanks necessary, Cassie," he said softly. "But I do want you to promise me you'll eat."

"I will. Promise."

"Good. And if it's real late when you're done and you want me to come and get you, just give me a call."

"I will, Beau. But honestly, that's not necessary." She laughed. "This is Cooper's Cove, remember? As safe a place as there ever was."

"True, but in case you change your mind and want some company, just call. I'll be here."

"I will," she said softly. "I will, Beau. And please tell Sofie I'm sorry, but it couldn't be helped."

"Cassie, stop feeling guilty," he said quietly. "You're a wonderful mother, totally devoted to your little girl. Once in a while these things happen, it's not like you're ignoring her or abandoning her. You're trying to earn a living to make both your lives better, and I think Sofie's smart enough to understand and respect that."

"I know." Cassie blew out a breath. "I know, Beau, but still I feel terribly guilty for missing tonight."

"Don't. I promise you Sofie will be so busy with her friends and the science project and the pizza that she won't have time to miss you. Now don't worry, Cass. I've got things handled on this end, so you handle your end and everything will be fine."

"You think so?" she said wearily.

"I know so. Now get back to work. I'm going to call Carm's right now. And don't forget what I said, if you want some company later just give me a call."

"I will, Beau," she promised. "I will."

Cassie hung up the phone then merely sat there for a moment. She was certain of it now. Beau had managed to completely steal her heart.

When someone knocked at the back door, Cassie assumed it was someone from Carm's delivering her dinner. She hadn't even thought about food until Beau mentioned it, and now her stomach was growling in anticipation.

She yanked open the back door with a smile that all but froze on her face when she saw the well-dressed male stranger shadowed in the darkness.

"Can I help you?" she asked, feeling the first thread of apprehension slide over her.

"Hello, Cassie." The stranger stepped past her and into the salon, shutting the door firmly behind him.

For a moment, Cassie could only stare, but then suddenly something about him seemed familiar and she gasped as time stood still and her mind raced to place his voice.

When the name came, her knees almost buckled in fear.

"Stephen," she whispered, shaken to the core. He was

the last person she ever expected to see again. The last person she ever expected to walk into her shop.

"Well, Cassie, I can see that time has been good to you." His gaze slid over her in a way that made a corresponding shudder race over her. "You're even more beautiful now than you were then."

"What do you want?" she finally managed to ask, cursing herself because her voice was quivering as much as her stomach.

She wasn't going to let him scare her, she told herself. There was nothing he could do to her. *Nothing.* Not anymore. She'd made certain of it.

Stephen walked past her into the shop, looking around. "You've got yourself a cute little business here," he said, his deep voice condescending, immediately sparking her temper.

She would not let him demean what she'd worked so many years for. She simply wouldn't.

"What do you want, Stephen?" she asked again, rubbing her hands up and down her suddenly chilled arms. "You're not welcome or wanted here."

He turned to her. "Really? Well, that's a shame, Cassie. Considering all we were to one another."

"What do you want?" she repeated again.

He turned to her, took a step closer and she backed away, until her back was pressed against one of the empty salon chairs. "I want to see my daughter," he said casually and Cassie stiffened.

"You don't have a daughter, remember?" she snapped. Her heart was racing with a fear so strong, she thought she might actually faint. But she couldn't. She had to hang on and be strong, to prove to him that he no longer had the power to manipulate her or threaten her.

Sofie was hers. Hers. And she'd do everything in her power to make certain nothing of this man ever touched or tainted her precious daughter.

"On the contrary," he said, pulling a newspaper clipping out of his overcoat pocket and unfolding it. It was the story and picture of Sofie and her friends and their science project from the *Cooper's Cove Carrier*. "It says here that my daughter, Sofie…" One brow rose and he glanced up at her. "Nice name. Not one I would have chosen, but then again I wasn't consulted," he said with a smug smile. "It says right here in this newspaper article that Sofie is entering a replica of the solar system in the science fair." He unfolded the article until the picture of Sofie was revealed. "She's a beautiful child, Cassie. Very photogenic. Always an asset in a political family."

The shivers ran deeper now, all the way to Cassie's heart. "She's not part of a political family," she corrected firmly. "She's part of my family."

"Yes, unfortunately she is."

Something about the way he talked about Sofie had Cassie all but cringing. "And she is beautiful, Stephen, but she's not your child, she's mine. All mine." She wasn't seventeen any longer, and she wasn't about to let him intimidate her or bully her. Not him. Not his father. Not his money.

"No need to get huffy, Cassie. The only reason I'm here is because I need to borrow Sofie for a few days."

"*Borrow* her?" she repeated dully. Cassie merely blinked at him in confusion, certain he was mad. "She's not a cup of sugar, Stephen. She's a child. *My* child."

"A mere technicality that can be easily remedied, Cassie," he said in a way that had her heart thrumming wildly again with fear. "I'm sure you're aware of my father's powerful political machine. It seems my father and some of his friends have put together an exploratory committee to test the viability of my candidacy for the United States Senate." He smiled and she wondered why she'd never noticed how cold his eyes were. Like a doll's. Dead. Lifeless.

"You have to admit, I am the perfect candidate. Wealthy, privileged, from a good family with a stellar pedigree. I've got a beautiful, perfect wife and a beautiful, perfect life. Unfortunately, there's just one thing missing."

"Your soul?"

He smiled, but there was no warmth, no humor in it. "Cute, Cassie. Very cute. But then you always did have a smart mouth." He glanced down at Sofie's picture and Cassie wanted to snatch it out of his hands. "No, Cassie, what's missing is a child. A family. You see, as perfect as my wife is, unfortunately the woman's barren. A fact that eluded me before our marriage or obviously I wouldn't have married her."

"So your perfect wife isn't so perfect after all." For some reason she felt a rush of sympathy for the poor woman who'd be saddled with this monster for life.

He smiled. "No, but she has other qualities, Cassie, including an impeccable name and an enormous trust fund that's going to help fund my political future." He sighed and stepped even closer, causing Cassie to rear back. "I have everything I need to project the image of the perfect candidate, except a family. Children. And trust me, in this day and age, a child is an absolute necessity for a politician. Voters want to look at a candidate and confirm, 'hey, he's just like me.' So what I need is to borrow Sofie for a few days. A week at best. We'll have a few family photographs taken, she'll appear at several fund-raisers with me, and we'll make sure her image is captured by all the television cameras so voters can see that hey, I really am just like them."

"You're joking, right?" Unable to totally comprehend what he was telling her, simply because it was so ludicrous, Cassie pressed her fingers to her tired, throbbing eyes, trying to make sense of this. "You're telling me you want to *borrow my daughter* to use as some kind of…*photo prop* for your political campaign?"

Every maternal instinct she had raced to the surface, and Cassie knew she would stop at nothing, absolutely nothing to keep this man away from her daughter.

"Don't be so melodramatic, Cassie. It really doesn't suit you." He touched her chin and she cringed away from him.

"Don't touch me," she said, hate burning in her eyes, wondering how on earth she'd ever welcomed or wanted his touch. "Don't ever touch me again."

He merely smiled. "You once welcomed my touch. Begged for it, as I recall."

"Get out," she snapped, clenching her hands into fists at her sides. "Get out of my shop and out of my life. *Now.*"

"I'm afraid I can't do that, Cassie. Not until I get what I came for. You see, Cassie you've had…" He had to glance down at the paper for the child's name. "Sofie, is it—for her whole life. I'm merely asking for a few days, maybe a week of her time. As her father I'm sure you can see that I'm entitled to at least that. And I'll certainly make it worth your while."

Temper all but hazed her vision. "You are *not* her father," she repeated again, realizing her voice was on the verge of hysteria. "And you're not entitled to anything. Do you really think I'd even let you near my daughter? Especially to use as some kind of prop to make *you* look good?" She laughed but the sound held no humor. "Not in this lifetime, buster."

"You don't have to put it in such vulgar terms." He glanced around. "From the looks of this dump it looks like you could use a fresh influx of cash."

Unable to control herself, Cassie's temper shot overboard. She shoved at his chest, nearly sending him sprawling on his back.

"You bastard! How dare you?" she seethed, stepping closer to him and causing him to take a cautious step back. "How dare you insult me or my child. You think I want or care about your money? You think I want or care about your silly little political future? I couldn't care less if you drowned in Cooper's Cove Lake." She shoved him again. "Now get out of my shop." She snatched Sofie's picture out of his hand and shoved it in her uniform pocket. She didn't want him even touching her daughter's picture. "And get out of my life. *Now!* And I swear to you if you ever approach my daughter, ever try to contact or see her, I'll make you sorry you were ever born."

"You're threatening me, Cassie?" He laughed wickedly. "That's really not a wise thing to do." He moved so fast she had no time to react. He grabbed a hunk of her hair and yanked her face to within inches of his. "In case you haven't learned, Cassie, I'm a Caldwell, and we always get what we want." Her vision blurred as he yanked harder and tears filled her eyes. But she refused to cry out, refused to give him the satisfaction of knowing he'd hurt her once again.

Wincing in pain, Cassie swung her free hand, putting

the weight of her body behind it. Her open hand smacked him hard against his cheek and ear, and he jerked back, allowing her to pull free of him.

"You bitch," he hissed, rubbing his face as she reached behind her for her cutting shears and held them up in front of her.

"Get out!" she screamed. "Get out of my shop right now before I call the police."

He glared at her for a moment, rubbing his red cheek and ear. "I'll leave, Cassie. But this isn't over. Not by a long shot. I promise you, you will be sorry. Nobody defies me and gets away with it, you hear me? Nobody." With that he stormed toward the back door, slamming it soundly behind him.

Cassie ran after him, locking the door and checking it several times to make sure it was locked. Then the firestorm of nerves and adrenaline seeped out of her and she began to shiver, her body shaking almost convulsively. Her breath hitched once, twice, then she sank to the floor, raised shaking hands to her face and let the tears flow.

The next day, Cassie still couldn't stop shaking. She hadn't slept a wink all night, and she had a horrific headache she couldn't get rid of, probably a combination of Stephen yanking her hair so hard and her own nerves. She'd finally gotten up and gone into the salon as soon as Sofie left for school.

In some ways it seemed as if last night had been a dream, but then Cassie touched the bump on the back of her head where Stephen had yanked her hair and realized it wasn't a dream; it was a nightmare and all too real.

She hadn't yet told anyone what had happened. She couldn't. She needed to process everything and deal with

the enormous shame she felt for allowing Stephen to terrorize her once again.

She also had to work through the fear. As much as she
thought she was beyond being scared by Stephen or his
family, the truth of the matter was that as long as Sofie was
vulnerable, Cassie knew she was going to be afraid of them.

Just as a precaution, she thought about calling Lucas,
who happened to be not just Katie's new husband, but also
the new police chief as well. She didn't expect anything
to come of it though. She already knew you couldn't arrest
someone for making a vague threat toward you. If you
could she'd have had both Stephen and his father arrested
years ago. No, the cops couldn't do anything unless
Stephen actually did something. And that was her greatest
fear: what he'd do next.

Stephen wasn't used to being told no. He wasn't used
to not getting everything he wanted and desired. But she'd
die before she allowed him access to her child, especially
to use as some kind of prop in a political campaign.

It was not knowing what he was going to do next that
had put her on edge because she'd learned in the past that
when Stephen wanted something, neither he nor his father
would stop at anything to get it.

Taking a deep breath to try to calm herself, Cassie knew
what she had to do. Ignoring her own fears, she walked
back to the salon and straight toward the reception desk.
She picked up the phone and called the police station and
asked for Lucas.

"Cassie." Stella, her new stylist, was watching her in the
mirror. "If you don't stop that pacing you're going to wear
out the linoleum."

"I know, I know, I'm sorry," Cassie said, dropping into an empty styling chair. "But I called Lucas almost a half an hour ago. Why hasn't he called me back?"

"Hon, they told you he was out on an emergency call." Stella smiled in sympathy. "He'll call you as soon as he gets back, I'm sure of it. So stop worrying."

Cassie nodded. Now that she'd made the call she just wanted to get this over. Once she called Lucas she found that she'd stopped shaking. Some of the fear still remained, but it wasn't quite so bad.

She just kept going over and over in her mind what she wanted to tell him, knowing she'd have to tell him the whole sordid story from beginning to end. She wasn't looking forward to it, but it was better than simply letting Stephen think he could terrorize her for the rest of her life.

"Well, lookee here," Stella said. "Here comes Lucas now. And Beau," Stella added with a frown.

Cassie jumped to her feet, wondering what Beau was doing here. Her heart began to beat frantically, not certain how he'd react when he learned what had happened.

"Cassie," Lucas said the moment he pushed through the door with Beau on his heels. "We need to talk to you."

Cassie's gaze went from one to the other. "I need to talk to you, too, Lucas. Did you get my message?"

"Message?" Lucas shook his head with a frown. "No, I'm sorry, I've been out of the office on an emergency."

Suddenly fearful and not certain why, Cassie moved closer to him. He looked paler than she'd ever seen him. "If you didn't get my message then what do you want to talk to me about?"

"Cass," Beau stepped forward and put his arms around her. "We have something to tell you."

Fear shot through her like adrenaline. "Something's wrong," she said instinctively, her voice edging upward in panic. "Oh, God, something's wrong, isn't it?" Her mind raced as tears flooded her eyes. "Mama? Did something happen to Mama?" she asked, her gaze frantically going from one to the other.

"Your mother's fine," Lucas said quietly. He and Beau exchanged glances before Lucas continued. "Cassie, we just came from the school."

"The school?" Her knees started to buckle, but Beau caught her. "Oh, God, Sofie. Something's happened to Sofie," she sobbed, unable to control her tears or her emotion.

"Cassie, honey, I'm sorry, but we think Sofie's been abducted."

"Oh, my God," Cassie cried. Now her knees did buckle and Beau helped her to the back room so they could have some privacy, carefully helping her into a chair. "What happened?" she demanded.

"Sofie was outside waiting for the bell to ring to start classes," Lucas began. "She was playing with Timmy and Brian, but when the bell rang to go inside, Sofie never made it inside. The boys couldn't find her and they told their teacher."

"I was up at the school," Beau added. "This is the week we do the annual vision and hearing exams. I was just getting things set up when Sofie's teacher came to see if Sofie was with me. She wasn't," he said, dragging a hand through his hair and looking more worried than Cassie had ever seen him. "I told her to call Lucas and I started searching the school but Sofie was nowhere to be found."

"Cassie, I've got every man on the force out combing

the town," Lucas said. "I've called for volunteers, and put out a nationwide Amber alert." He patted her trembling hand. "We'll find her, Cass, I promise." His words were firm. "You have my word on it."

"I think I know who took her." Fists clenched, tears streamed down Cassie's face.

"Who, Cassie?"

Her eyes closed for a moment. "Her father."

"Cassie," Beau stood up, shocked. His face had drained of all color. "Has Stephen contacted you?"

"Yes," she whispered, unable to look at him. "He came here late last night."

"Why didn't you tell me?" Beau demanded, his temper showing. "Why the hell didn't you tell me he was bothering you again?" He shook his head. "When did this happen, Cassie? When?"

"Last night, I said." Cassie shook her head. "Late. I couldn't tell you, Beau." She raised stricken, swollen eyes to his. "I simply couldn't." She saw the way her words struck him, like individual knives cutting into his heart and knew he'd never understand that she'd kept this from him not because she didn't trust him but because she was trying to protect him.

"I thought you trusted me," Beau said quietly, unable to keep the hurt from his voice. "I thought I'd finally earned your trust."

"I do trust you," she whispered. "I do, but I couldn't tell anyone. I was too ashamed and afraid," she admitted as tears streaked down her face. "He threatened me, Lucas, because I refused to allow him to *rent* Sofie for a few days to make potential voters think he was a family man."

"What?" Beau merely stared at her in shock. "He

wanted to *rent* Sofie like she was a piece of furniture or something? And you didn't think that was important to tell me, Cass?" The growing disappointment in Beau's eyes tore her heart apart. "Cassie," Beau said quietly. "Just because I'm not Sofie's biological father doesn't mean I don't love or care for her. I couldn't love that child more if she was mine. You should have told me he was here harassing you. You simply should have trusted me enough to tell me." He lifted stricken eyes to hers. "If you'd trusted me, maybe we could have prevented this from happening."

"I'm sorry." She couldn't think, the fear was too strong. Her helpless little girl was with a madman and she simply couldn't think of anything else.

"Beau." Lucas stood up. "Can we deal with why Cassie didn't tell you, later?" he said, giving Beau a look. "Right now I need to know everything about Sofie's father." He turned to Cassie, who'd curled up in a ball in the chair. "I want you to tell me everything, Cassie, and don't leave anything out."

Swallowing hard, she told Lucas the name of Sofie's father and that he had never before had any contact with his daughter. When she got to Stephen's latest visit, and explained again how he had wanted to *rent* Sofie so he'd look good for his upcoming campaign, she heard Beau swear viciously and storm out of the room.

"Beau," she called, her voice weepy, but Lucas put a gentle hand on her arm.

"Cassie, let him go. He's hurt and angry right now and more than a little scared. He loves Sofie like she was his own, and trust me, I know how that is. You need to give him some time to cool down." He took her hand and forced a smile. "Do you think you can do that, Cass? Just give him some time and space."

"Yes," she whispered, her stomach churning in fear. But this fear was different, this fear was that she'd lost Beau forever.

"Cassie, who has legal custody of Sofie?" Lucas asked gently.

"I do," she said firmly. "Stephen signed a paper declaring he was not her birth father. So legally he has no rights to her nor is he any legal relation. He was little more than a sperm donor."

Lucas shook his head. "I don't understand, Cass."

She sighed. "I was seventeen when I got pregnant and Stephen's father, former Senator Caldwell, threatened to destroy me if I didn't sign something stating that Stephen wasn't Sofie's biological father."

"And you did?"

She nodded.

"Do you still have that paper?"

"It's in my safe-deposit box at the bank."

"So Stephen Caldwell legally has no parental rights to Sofie?"

"Absolutely none," she stated firmly. "He has no rights when it comes to me or Sofie."

Lucas nodded. "Good, that way I can arrest him for kidnapping. In this state even if he can prove he *is* the birth father, it doesn't matter. If he doesn't have legal custody of Sofie or even visitation rights, technically it's a kidnapping. And Cassie, let me assure you it will be a long time before Stephen Caldwell sees the light of day once I get through with him."

Frightened, she laid a hand on Lucas's arm. "Lucas, be careful. His father is a very wealthy, powerful man. If you dare to do anything to his son, he'll come after you. That's why I didn't tell Beau. I didn't want to drag him into this mess and perhaps have Stephen's father come after him."

"I understand that, Cass, but I'm afraid Beau doesn't. All he knows is that you didn't trust him enough to tell him. When a man loves a woman, and her child, he's very protective of them. And Beau is not only hurt right now, he's also furious that he wasn't able to protect you both. He feels as if he's failed you and Sofie and that's a whole lot for a man with a good sized ego to handle. It's going to take some time to heal so you're going to have to be patient."

"You…you think Beau…loves us?" she asked, stunned, and Lucas grinned.

"Cassie, everyone can see it, except probably you." He patted her hand. "You two will have to work this out, but right now, I need to focus on Sofie."

Cassie closed her eyes and held the thought that Beau loved her and Sofie close to her heart. Even if it wasn't true, right now it was the only hopeful thing she had.

"Be careful, Lucas, please?" she pleaded, laying a hand on his arm.

He patted her hand to reassure her. "Cassie, I've dealt with much worse than Stephen Caldwell in my time. And a man who is reduced to snatching a child for his own stupid political purposes isn't exactly the brightest flame in the fireplace. He did a very stupid thing, today, Cassie. And I guarantee you I'm going to put him behind bars for a very long time for it. Nowadays the court takes a very dim view of men who abduct children."

"But Lucas, his father—"

"Let me worry about his father," he said quietly.

She nodded mutely, absently tearing the tissue in her hands into bits and pieces.

"Cassie, I want you to think. Where do you think Stephen would have taken Sofie? Does he have a house or an office somewhere near Cooper's Cove?"

She pressed her hand to her forehead. "His family has a fishing compound, sort of a huge fishing lodge, on the other side of Cooper's Cove Lake. You can't miss it, it's that huge brick-and-stone structure jutting out over the pier. I believe Stephen's father and mother still live there for part of the year."

"Okay," Lucas said, jotting it down. "Now, is there anything else you can tell me?"

"No, just that I think Stephen is truly dangerous."

"Not nearly as dangerous as Beau and I will be if he hurts one hair on Sofie's head." Lucas stood up. "I'll keep in touch, Cassie. Stay here. And if you hear from Stephen or Sofie let me know right away."

She nodded, twisting her tissue impotently in her hand. "I will, Lucas, I promise."

Chapter Ten

"Beau," Lucas said as they walked up the paved drive of the Caldwell fishing lodge. It was a roughhewn three-story stone-and-brick mansion that looked out of place among the small, cozy family cabins lining the shore. "I know your emotions are all tangled up right now. You're hurt, angry and frustrated, but we still have to do things by the book. So let me handle this." Beau's face was drawn, his lips grim, his eyes filled with a fire that wasn't hard to read. The man was ready to tear Caldwell limb from limb, Lucas decided, realizing he just might let him. "I'm a cop, Beau, but you're a civilian, and I don't want to have to haul you in right behind Caldwell. Or fend off a police brutality complaint." He put his hand on Beau's arm. "Do you understand me? Everything has to be by the book."

"I understand," Beau snapped grimly as they approached the door. There was a raging firestorm inside of him, one unlike anything he'd ever felt before. This Caldwell character had laid his hands on Cassie, hurt her, bruised her and scared her, and for that alone he could kill the man. But snatching Sofie, taking that little girl away from those who loved her and probably scaring her to death, was incomprehensible. He hoped the man would rot in hell for what he did to Sofie and Cassie.

Lucas rang the bell and heard the resounding peal inside. He and Beau exchanged glances before Lucas rang the bell a second time. Finally they heard some life inside.

The heavy wooden door was pulled open by a disheveled man dressed in slacks and a wrinkled shirt. There were two long red scratches on his face and his hair looked like he'd gotten caught in a wind tunnel. He appeared both annoyed and frustrated by the intrusion. "Yes, what do you want?" he snapped, looking from Lucas to Beau, then clearly dismissing them.

"Are you Stephen Caldwell?" Lucas asked, and Stephen scowled at him.

"What the hell business is it of yours?" He started to shut the door again, but Beau wedged his foot in between the door and the jamb.

"I'm Lucas Porter, chief of police of Cooper's Cove." Lucas flashed his badge. "Now, are you Stephen Caldwell or not?"

"Yes, yes. Not that it's any of your business. Now what do you want? I'm a busy man."

"We're investigating the abduction of a little girl, Sofie Miller, and we'd like to know if you have any information regarding her whereabouts."

Stephen's face went ashen. "Never heard of her, now I'm busy. Leave me alone." He started to shut the door, but something caught Beau's eye. He reached for Stephen's hand, yanking it forward.

"Lucas, these are fresh bite marks. *Human* bite marks," Beau clarified, inspecting the red, inflamed little marks more closely. "Made by a child judging from the size of them." As a pediatrician, he'd treated his fair share of child bite marks. Their mark was very distinctive and he had no doubt these marks had been made by Sofie.

"Unhand me," Stephen demanded, struggling to dislodge his hand from Beau's grip.

"He's got Sofie," Beau said firmly, giving Stephen's hand a hard yank, and pulling the man off balance so he fell forward. Beau's other hand was waiting, fisted, and caught Stephen right on the chin. His eyes rolled and then he slid soundlessly to the ground.

"Such a shame he's so clumsy, fell right into that one," Lucas said with a shake of his head. "Go on in, Beau. Go find Sofie. I'll take care of the trash," he said, giving Stephen Caldwell an absent nudge with the steel toe of his boot.

Beau charged through the front door, his knuckles burning, his heart tripping. "Sofie!" Beau called, racing in. "It's Dr. Beau, honey, everything's fine. I came to take you home. Sofie? Where are you, honey? Sofie!"

"Up here, Dr. Beau. I'm up here." She was standing, peering over the railing. When she saw him, she grinned and started bouncing in excitement. "I'm up here, right here." She waved her little hand at him and he had to swallow the lump in his throat. Her barrettes were long gone and her hair was a mess. Her tights drooped around her knees and ankles and she only had on one shoe, but he'd never seen a more beautiful sight in his life.

"Sofie!" Beau took the stairs two at a time. "Oh, my

God, Sofie." He scooped her into his arms, holding her tight against him, wanting to reassure himself that she was safe. "I was so scared, honey. So scared. Did he hurt you?" Beau asked, drawing back to look at her dirt smudged face.

"He pulled my hair," Sofie complained with a scowl, rubbing her sore head. "That bad man pulled my hair. So I bit him," she said, making Beau throw back his head and roar with laughter. "I don't like him, Dr. Beau. He's not nice." She placed her little hands on either side of Beau's face, her eyes filled with absolute trust and unbelievable love. "I knew you'd come and get me. I just knew it, Dr. Beau."

"Oh, God, Sofie." He held her close, burying his face in her hair, his heart aching with a love so profound he wasn't certain his body was big enough to hold it.

"I love you, Dr. Beau," Sofie said, wrapping skinny trusting arms around his neck. "Lots," she added, giving him a kiss on the cheek.

"I love you, too, sweetheart." He kissed her back, making her grin. "Lots, too."

She scowled suddenly and rubbed her aching head again. "Could we go home now? I'm kinda tired and my head hurts."

"Yes, sweetheart," he said, burying his face in her hair and taking the first decent breath since he'd heard she was missing. "We're going home."

Cassie was pacing a path in the linoleum of the shop again. Lucas had called almost a half an hour ago to tell her they'd found Sofie safe and sound. And arrested Stephen on numerous charges, including kidnapping. But she couldn't take any joy from that, not until she had her daughter in her arms once again. Waiting for Lucas to bring Sofie back seemed to be interminable.

"You know," Gracie began solemnly, nestling closer to Jasper in one of the chairs in the salon. "I should have put a curse on that awful man years ago."

Cassie stopped her pacing and turned to her mother. "Mama? Do you *really* know how to do that?" she asked nervously, resisting an urge to shiver at the mere thought of her mother going around putting curses on people. "Put a curse on someone?"

Gracie sighed and clutched Jasper's hand tighter. "No, dear, unfortunately I don't. But it would really be a useful skill to have, especially at times like this, don't you think?" she asked, brightening.

"Oh, yeah," Cassie muttered. "About as useful as a third foot."

"Aye, don't be alarmed," Jasper said with a smile. "Your mum's just feeling a bit frustrated that she didn't see this coming and couldn't have done something to prevent it." Jasper lifted Gracie's hand for a kiss. "You know she adores the little princess, as do I. 'Tis a terrible thing when someone takes out their frustrations on a helpless child. 'Tis a good thing I don't remember how to perform any Druid's magic, or I'd have been tempted to weave a bit of dark magic of my own on that rascal."

"Druid's magic?" Cassie repeated in horror. She raised a shaky hand in the air. "Uh…Uncle Jasper, Mama, please, no curses. No Druid's magic. And definitely no spells." She had enough trouble handling *earthly* problems. "And Mama, please, please don't feel guilty. This is not your fault. It's Stephen's fault and no one else's."

Cassie whirled when the bell over the door tinkled and

Beau walked in carrying a very disheveled but happy little girl in his arms.

"Mama!"

"Sofie." Cassie ran to her, tears running down her face.

"Mama," Sofie cried, reaching out her arms to her mother. Cassie grabbed her, then hugged her tight, burying her face in Sofie's hair. She merely held Sofie and sobbed, so grateful her child was safe, trying to banish the awful fear that had nearly paralyzed her. Sofie was home and safe and that's all that mattered.

"Mama, you're squishing me," Sofie finally complained, trying to wiggle free. "I can't breathe."

Laughing, Cassie loosened her hold and brushed Sofie's tangled hair out of her face. "Are you all right, honey? Did he hurt you?"

Sofie scowled and rubbed the back of her head. "That bad man pulled my hair, Mama. And I wouldn't get into his car, Mama, 'cuz he's a stranger, and I know not to go anywhere with strangers. But he grabbed me by my hair and dragged me to the car. I lost my shoe and I yelled and kicked, but he wouldn't let me go so…I…bit him."

"Good for you, princess," Jasper said, holding Gracie's hand as they approached. "Aye, I'd have been happy if you'd given him a bite for me and your grandma as well."

"Mama, that bad man said he was my daddy," Sofie said with another scowl. "He's not my daddy, is he?"

Cassie's gaze met Beau's, her heart suddenly tripping in fear. She knew one day Sofie would want to know about her father, but Cassie had no idea what to tell her. Especially now. She never wanted her daughter to know that Stephen Caldwell was her father, because he wasn't, not in the real sense of the word. As far as she was concerned,

Stephen Caldwell was nothing more than what she'd told Lucas: a sperm donor.

Beau met her gaze for the first time since he'd entered the salon, saw the uncertainty and fear in Cassie's eyes and gave her a small smile.

"Sofie," Beau said gently. "Do you know what a daddy is?"

She thought about it for a moment, then frowned a bit. "Well, not really 'cuz I never had a daddy, Dr. Beau."

He nodded, then smiled, taking one of her hands in his. "You see, Sofie, a daddy is someone who loves you with all his heart. He protects you and looks after you and is always there for you."

"Does he help you with homework and have dinner with you, and have sleepovers at your house every night like Rusty's dad does?"

"Yep. A dad does all those things. But most important, Sofie, a dad never, ever hurts or frightens his child."

"And he doesn't pull her hair, either, right, Dr. Beau?" Sofie asked, rubbing the back of her head again.

"No, sweetheart, he definitely doesn't pull your hair. A dad protects and loves his child and is involved in every part of his child's life." He hesitated. "He tucks her in at night, and helps her say her prayers. He goes on field trips and meets her friends and teaches her to ride a bike and climb a tree, and all kinds of wonderful things. A father is a little girl's very best friend and does anything and everything he can to make her happy. So now that you know what a father is, Sofie, do *you* think the bad man is your father?"

"Uh-uh," Sofie said, shaking her head and Cassie let out a sigh of relief and mouthed a silent thank-you to Beau.

"But Dr. Beau, do you think I could have you for my daddy then? I asked mama to ask you but I think she forgot. But I think you should be my daddy 'cuz you do all that stuff for me, and you don't ever pull my hair, and you help me with my school work and my science project and other stuff, and I love you, and you love me. So could you be my daddy?" Sofie's big brown eyes, wide and innocent, met his and she placed her little hands on his cheeks again. "Please, Dr. Beau, 'cuz I love you, Dr. Beau. Lots and lots. And Mama loves you, too, don't you, Mama?"

Cassie stood there, flushing pink, aware that everyone, especially her daughter, was looking at her, waiting for an answer.

"Mama, you do love Dr. Beau, don't you?" Sofie prompted again, her voice so hopeful Cassie wanted to cry.

"Yes, honey," she finally admitted, unable to look at Beau. She sighed. "I love Dr. Beau, too." She realized she'd never said a truer statement in her life. "Lots and lots," she added with a smile. "You're right."

"See, Dr. Beau, and Grandma loves you, too, right, Grandma?"

Gracie beamed at her granddaughter. "Well of course I love Dr. Beau, dear. Everyone does," she added with a tender smile for him.

"So see, Dr. Beau, we all love you. So do you want to be my daddy?" Eyes hopeful, Sofie waited, watching him. "You could live with us. We could all live together, just like Rusty's dad lives with him."

"Well, sweetheart, to tell you the truth, I'd love to be your daddy. And I'd be so proud to have you for my daughter. But would you mind if your mom and I just talked about this a bit? You see, if I'm going to be your daddy, that means I'm also going to be your mama's husband so I think that's something she needs to have a say in."

"Oh." Sofie's face fell for a moment, then she brightened suddenly. "Okay, you and Mama talk about it, then you can be my daddy, okay?"

Beau laughed and kissed her forehead. "You've got yourself a deal."

Beau insisted on taking Sofie to his office for a complete physical exam just to be on the safe side. Although he was certain she remained unhurt besides for her sore head, he wanted a thorough examination on record to be used in court if necessary. Once he was absolutely certain Sofie was fine, he allowed her to go home with Cassie. Sofie and Cassie invited him to go with them, but he needed some time to think.

He was emotionally drained from the day's events, and still smarting over the knowledge that Cassie hadn't trusted him enough to tell him about Stephen's visit. He simply didn't understand it. He thought she knew him well enough by now to know she could trust him—with her life and her daughter's.

Cassie had said she loved him, but what he didn't know was if she'd said that merely because Sofie had put her on the spot. He didn't want Cassie declaring her love for him simply because Sofie wanted him for a dad and she wanted to please her daughter.

He finally realized he wanted—needed—Cassie's love, wanted and needed her in his life, as his wife. Not just for today, but forever. Simply because he loved her in return. More than anything in the world.

As he walked aimlessly through his office, trying to find

something to do with himself, he realized one thing for certain: Cassie might love him, but she didn't trust him. And he knew from experience that without trust, love couldn't grow or blossom.

When a knock sounded at the back door, Beau frowned, glanced at his watch, then went to answer it. It was a bit late for patients, but then again, it could be an emergency.

He yanked open the door, surprised to find Shorty and Rusty and Sean.

"Aye Boss, we've got a little…situation here, one I thought you should be aware of," Shorty said, with a none-too-subtle nod toward the boys.

"Come on in, then," Beau said, stepping back to let all three of them in. He led them through the hallway to his private office and offered them all a seat. "Okay, Shorty, so what's up?"

Shorty frowned. "Well, Boss, 'tis like this. I was at home, puttering in my greenhouse because it relaxes me so." He shook his head. "We've all had quite a shock today with what happened with the little princess. And we're all grateful she's safe and sound." Shorty had to clear the lump from his throat. "Anyways, I was in the greenhouse when these two lads showed up with a message for me." Shorty scratched his head. "And as soon as I read it, aye, I knew I had to come tell you about it."

"What was the message?"

Rusty and Sean exchanged glances then shrugged. "Dr. Beau, Aunt Cassie asked me to deliver this message to Mr. Shorty." Rusty pulled a wrinkled note out of his pocket and handed it to Beau across his desk.

Beau looked at Rusty skeptically as he opened the note and read it.

Dear Shorty:

I told you you'd be the first to know if I changed my mind about letting you keep me. I have. But if you're going to keep me, you have to keep Sofie as well. We're a package deal.

Love, Cassie

P.S. And just so you know, I can do a few parlor tricks of my own. I can cook! Really cook. From scratch.

"Soon as I read it, Boss, aye, I knew I'd better show it to you." Shorty leaned forward, his eyes gleaming, a smile on his face. "Can the lass really cook?" he asked and Beau nodded.

"Oh, yeah, Shorty. Cassie can cook like nobody's business."

"Aye, then is it settled, Boss? We're gonna keep her?"

Beau laughed. "Oh yeah, Shorty, we're gonna keep her." With his heart soaring, he looked at the boys. "And boys, thanks." Beau reached in his pocket and tugged free two bills, handing them to the boys across the desk.

Rusty and Sean's eyes widened. "Gee, Dr. Beau, what's this for?" Rusty asked as he eyed the enormous bill.

"It's a tip, Rusty. You have no idea how much I appreciate you delivering that message."

"Uh…then…Dr. Beau, maybe we'd better tell you we have another note to deliver to your uncle Jasper. Do you want to see it?" Beau nodded and Rusty fished the note out of his pocket. "Here."

Not wanting to be left out, Shorty leaned forward. "Aye, Boss, what does the note say?"

Beau unfolded the note and read it.

"Uncle Jasper:
It won't be necessary for you to try to find a match for
Beau, since I've found one for him. If you approve, I'd
like to be his match—for life, and the one to give Beau
a wee little Bradford heir. That is, if he'll have me.
Love, Cassie"

"Aye Boss, does this mean what I think it means?"
Shorty asked with a lift of his brow and Beau nodded,
getting to his feet.

"I hope so, Shorty. I hope so." Beau grabbed his coat
off the rack. "Shorty, see that the boys get home safely."

"Aye, I can do that," Shorty said, herding the boys
toward the hall. "And aye, I'll be wishing good luck to you,
too, Boss."

"Thanks, Shorty." Beau had a feeling he was going to
need it.

Cassie sighed as she walked out on the back porch and
breathed deeply of the fresh spring air. She'd finally gotten
Sofie down for the night. She was a little scared alone in
her bedroom so Cassie had lain with her until she fell asleep.

When Gracie offered to relieve her, Cassie reluctantly
agreed. Her nerves were still shot and she'd yet to stop
shaking.

Sitting on the porch swing Cassie merely stared at the
darkened sky. Rusty and Sean should have delivered her
notes by now, and she was hoping Beau would come over.

She needed to talk to him, to explain to him exactly why
she hadn't told him about Stephen. It had nothing to do

with trust, and everything to do with her own feelings of fear and shame.

"Cassie?"

Beau's voice in the sudden darkness startled her. "I'm back here, on the swing," she said, her pulse skipping at just the sound of his voice.

He came around the porch and merely stopped to look at her before climbing the four steps to her.

"It's nice out here," he said, sitting down.

"Now that the weather's finally decent," she admitted, stalling for time. She took a deep breath. "Beau," she began softly. "I need to explain something to you." She turned to him, saw the hopeful look in his eye and felt hope herself. Her heart was so full of love and sorrow for the pain she caused him she wasn't certain she could properly explain it to him.

"I didn't tell you about Stephen's visit or his threats because…because I was ashamed and afraid, not because I didn't trust you." She reached for his hands, wanting to feel his warmth, his steadiness. "It never occurred to me that by *not* telling you, you'd think I didn't trust you. I was ashamed to tell you I'd let him frighten me again, and I was afraid if I told anyone about what he'd done, it would only make things worse. You don't know him, Beau. He's truly not playing with a full deck."

"Cassie, you don't ever have to be afraid of anyone ever again. Not as long as I'm around." He took her hand, held it in his. "I don't know if you talked to Lucas yet or not?"

"No, not since he left the salon today." Her nerves skittered in alarm. "Lucas isn't going to let Stephen go, is he?"

Beau smiled. "Oh, no, Stephen's going to be facing

federal kidnapping charges." His smiled broadened. "You see, Stephen must have forgotten Cooper's Cove Lake encompasses two states, Wisconsin and Illinois, or else he's too stupid to think about it. When he crossed over the lake on his way to his father's fishing lodge, he crossed state lines. That's a federal offense. And there's not a thing his daddy's money or power can do to get him out of this one. Stephen's going to be away for a long, long time. And that isn't even counting the state charges Lucas is going to hit him with. He'll stand trial in a federal court, then be tried in a Wisconsin court, so Sofie will probably be old and gray before he ever sees the light of day again."

"Oh." Cassie pressed her hand to her mouth as tears filled her eyes. "I wish I could say I felt sorry for him, but I don't, Beau." She shook her head. "I simply don't."

"After what that man put you and your daughter through—not just now, but in the past as well—you shouldn't worry about feeling anything for him except maybe contempt." Beau kissed her hand. "Even if Stephen wasn't going to be wasting away in a federal facility you still wouldn't have anything to fear from him. Or anyone else." He laid his hand on her cheek. "Cassie, I love you, and I love Sofie with all my heart. But unless you can trust me, truly trust me, we don't have a future."

"I love you, Beau," she said taking a deep breath. "And I do trust you. With all of my heart and my life as well as my daughter's. And quite frankly, that's not something I ever thought I'd be able to do. I didn't think I could ever love or trust again. Truly. I had myself convinced it just wasn't possible, not after what Stephen had done to me. But day by day as I got to know you, as I got to see the true goodness in you, I realized that I was capable of loving and trusting again. And that scared me because I didn't know if you could ever love or trust in return."

He nodded, giving her hand a kiss. "I understand exactly how you feel. I was pretty sure I would never be able to trust another woman again, and then there are my fears about bringing a child into the world and worrying about subjecting it to the same painful childhood experiences as I had."

"Oh, Beau, Sofie just went through a small bout of it and look how helpful you were to her, how diligent and thoughtful you were, and how you used your own knowledge and experience to make it a much more positive experience for her. I have no doubt you'll do the same for our child. No matter what happens."

He nodded. "I really had resigned myself to being alone the rest of my life." He lifted a hand and tenderly brushed her hair off her face. "But then I ran into a little runaway girl and her skeptical, gun-shy mother and found that like it or not I was falling in love—with both of you."

"I love you too and this afternoon when Sofie asked you to be her father I realized that my little girl loves you. She couldn't love you more if you were her real father."

"But Cassie, I am her real father for all practical purposes," he insisted with a smile. "I meant everything I said about what a father is, when I explained it to Sofie. The man who does those things for a child is her real father no matter whose sperm produced her. I want to be Sofie's father, her only father, and that can't happen until we're married. I want to adopt Sofie, give her my name as well as my heart."

"Married?" Cassie repeated, stunned. She shook her head, wanting to be certain she'd heard him correctly. "You want me to marry you?"

"No," Beau corrected with a grin. "I want you *and* Sofie to marry me. The sooner the better."

"Then I say yes for both of us." And Cassie sealed it with a kiss.

A few minutes later, Beau leaned back and smiled. "Uh…Cassie, there's something I'd better tell you."

"Uh-oh," she laughed. "What now?"

"Uh…did I mention that I'm also Uncle Jasper's sole heir?"

"Sole heir?" she repeated nervously and he nodded.

"You know what that means?" he asked.

"More money?" she all but groaned, and he nodded again.

"Afraid so. Does that scare you, Cassie?"

"Well, that depends. Can we give it away?"

Beau shrugged. "Sure, I don't see why not."

She pressed her lips to his. "Then it doesn't scare me."

"Psst, Dr. Beau," Sofie whispered in a voice loud enough to be heard on the other side of town. "Does this mean you're gonna be my daddy?"

Beau turned and grinned at his future daughter, who had her face smashed up against the screen, listening. "Oh, yeah, honey, that's exactly what it means. I'm going to be your daddy and your mother's husband and anything and everything else either of you will ever need."

"All we need is you, Beau," Cassie whispered, resting her head against his shoulder, finally feeling totally whole and content. "Just you. Forever."

* * * * *

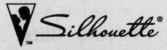

**The Scorsolini Princes:
proud rulers and passionate lovers
who need convenient wives!**

Welcome to this brand-new miniseries,
set in glamorous and exotic places—it's
a world filled with passion, romance and royals!

Don't miss this new trilogy by

Lucy Monroe

THE PRINCE'S VIRGIN WIFE
May 2006

HIS ROYAL LOVE-CHILD
June 2006

THE SCORSOLINI MARRIAGE BARGAIN
July 2006

www.eHarlequin.com   HPRB0506